# GODS REMEMBERED

# GODS REMEMBERED

## FORGOTTEN GODS™ BOOK EIGHT

ST BRANTON     CM RAYMOND     LE BARBANT

DISRUPTIVE IMAGINATION

Copyright © 2019 ST Branton, CM Raymond, and LE Barbant
Cover by http://www.bookcoverartistry.com/
Cover copyright © LMBPN Publishing

LMBPN Publishing
PMB 196, 2540 South Maryland Pkwy
Las Vegas, NV 89109

First US edition, January
Print ISBN: 978-1-64202-965-9

To Gavin, Hank, and Simone. May you find magic everywhere and causes worth fighting for.

**Thanks to the JIT Readers**

Angel LaVey
Larry Omans
Paul Westman
Misty Roa
Crystal Wren

*If we've missed anyone, please let us know!*

**Editor**

SkyHunter Editing Team

# PROLOGUE

The road he walked was shrouded in shadows. Ahead of him, the dark temple loomed against a malevolent, churning sky. With every step, the cries of the damned rang louder in his ears and every breath filled his nostrils with the stench of burning hair and flesh. Death surrounded him.

He welcomed it like the embrace of an old friend.

The man's hands hung at his sides and his fingertips dripped viscous scarlet. Whatever color his skin had been, it was of no consequence now. All that mattered was the crimson wash of blood that marked his trail toward the temple. He liked the way it felt as it pooled in the crevices of his palms and stiffened around his knuckles. The subtle sensations made everything real. He bowed his head slightly and a smile crept across his downturned face.

The front of the temple stood open to the acrid air. Great, soaring pillars lined the way to the elevated throne perched atop a flight of bone-white stairs. He could already see the lone figure that waited, slender and pale. A cloak of shadows wreathed the man's shoulders as he stood before the throne and his eyes pierced even through their darkness. His lip curled as the bloody figure approached the base of the steps and began to climb.

Perfect, round drops of blood anointed the stairway. The pilgrim crested the landing and bowed. "It is done, my lord." The words, though softly spoken, resounded through the structure.

The thin, curling smile widened. "Truly a noble sacrifice," said the lean figure. "But we both know there is one last thing to do." He withdrew one hand from behind his back, a knife clutched in his fingers. "Commit all to me and be reborn."

The pilgrim's breath caught in his throat—from exhilaration rather than fear. How long he had waited for such a glorious privilege? How hard he had toiled? How much blood he had shed?

So much blood.

The hand that held the dagger waited expectantly. He could feel the cloaked man's gaze upon him. He reached up and grasped the blade. At last, the time had come.

The pilgrim raised the knife to his breast and plunged it deep. More blood, fresh and warm, gushed over him. His hands sank deep into the wound and when they emerged, they held his own still-beating heart. He presented it to his venerated lord, both arms outstretched in total supplication.

Then, he collapsed. His body was nothing but a shell, an empty vessel and the remnant of his mortal life. Coldness spread as color leaked from the world that faded around him. He had wondered for a long time what it might be like to die, to face the end of all existence.

Now, he smiled as he slipped across some invisible threshold. He had been so very wrong. There was no end there.

No. This was, in fact, the grandest of beginnings.

# CHAPTER ONE

"I still can't believe you did that," Deacon said and shook his head. He walked toward me from the middle of the field outside Fort Victory, which we'd transformed into the world's least impressive shooting range. Fifty yards behind him, two bloated pumpkins and an arrangement of equally sorry-looking gourds adorned some tree stumps that protruded from the untended grass.

"What?" I asked and kicked at a clod of dirt. "I'm a damn decent public speaker these days if I do say so myself. Maybe I saw our big, messed-up family all gathered together in the cafeteria and the spirit of oration simply struck me out of the blue. 'Give me your huddled masses, yearning to breathe free,' and all that. Refugees are what inspiration is made of. I think it went well."

I was joking, but that wasn't too far from the truth. The enduring spirit of our ragtag band of brothers and sisters had filled me with hope and inspiration. That, and it was simply damn good to be home.

Of course, Delano's shadow still loomed large over the

new world order we constantly tried to cobble together out of mud and army rations. I felt like I needed to imbue my people with something that would keep them going. We all knew times would be tough for a while.

Deacon checked his gun. "Hey, I'm not knocking it," he said. "Badass, sexy Wonder Woman looks great on you." He leveled the pistol and looked down the sights.

I laughed. "You would be into Wonder Woman," I said.

He looked warily at me from the corner of his eye. "I'm afraid to ask what that means."

I punched him gently in the arm. "It means you have a giant boner for justice."

Deacon grinned. "Among other things."

"I walked into that one." I sighed and rolled my eyes. "Will you teach me how to shoot or not?" As much as I feigned annoyance, I couldn't keep the smile off my face and he knew it.

"The best way to teach," he said philosophically, "is by example. Observe." He drew in a breath, adjusted his stance, and squared his shoulders. On the exhale, he squeezed the trigger six times in rapid succession. Fifty yards away, pumpkin flesh erupted in thick orange ribbons. Seed shrapnel pummeled the ground around the stump. "There." He turned to me. "See? Easy as pie."

"Says the FBI agent with years of formal training," I retorted. "I guess it doesn't look so difficult." He cleared the gun, then handed it to me. I retrieved a full mag from my pocket and swapped it for the one Deacon had used. He watched me click it into place and rack the slide.

"So far, so good," he said. "Now, remember. It's all about

focus. You have to be able to work *with* the weapon instead of against it."

A familiar sentiment, but it wasn't the same. I felt like I brandished a movie prop. "Are we sure I can't simply use my sword?" I grumbled.

"The world was never saved by a lousy shot," Deacon quipped. "And you, gorgeous, are among the lousiest."

I frowned at him. "Take that back, St. Clare." I was willing to admit that my firearm skills needed work, but 'the lousiest' seemed like a stretch.

He smirked. "Make me." That said, he moved around behind me as I aimed the gun at my bulbous orange target. "Clear your mind. Focus everything down to one point— the point of entry. Don't tense up like that. Keep your shoulders loose." He moved my arm a little. "There. Breathe in, breathe out, and fire."

I tried to mimic everything I'd seen him do a minute earlier, but it felt all wrong. The gun might as well have been a toy in my hands. I missed the reassuring weight of the *Gladius Solis* and clean heft of its swing. Given the choice, I'd pick that damn blade every day of my life.

Still, the man had offered to teach me to shoot, and I wouldn't turn down any opportunity to be alone with him. Plus, things were quiet at the moment in the wake of our adventure out west. We had returned to a routine of team meetings, mess hall meals, and daily patrols. If I didn't do something, I'd run the risk of going stir crazy as I had before.

I sucked in my breath and as I exhaled, my trigger finger squeezed. The pistol jumped, and the smallest sliver of my pumpkin rocketed off into space.

"That counts," I said to Deacon. "I hit it. You saw that." I lowered the gun so I could point to the millimeter of exposed orange pumpkin meat.

"I don't know," he said doubtfully. "I think that's what we in the business like to call a technicality."

"Ugh." I scowled at the weapon. "You guys in the business can shove it up your asses." I raised the weapon once more and I took another shot. This second attempt went shamefully wide, even to my eyes. The bullet zinged off into the open sky.

"And that," said Deacon as he shifted my arm once more, "is why we practice in an open field in the middle of nowhere." He put his hands on my shoulders and squeezed gently. "Give it one more try."

I groaned but did as he suggested. The third bullet zipped over the pumpkin's stem and left its broad face completely undisturbed. Behind me, Deacon tried not to laugh. He succeeded—mostly.

I popped the magazine out and tossed it into the grass. Somehow, I resisted the urge to chuck the gun after it and placed it carefully on the ground beside me instead. "Fuck this shit!" The pistol had no sooner left my grip than I had my trusty sword in hand. I uttered a warrior's shout as I threw it in a forward arc. The blade stuck neatly, dead center in the target's body.

Deacon nodded and arched his eyebrows. "There we go. That's not bad at all."

"Can your stupid bullets do *this*?" I asked. On cue, the *Gladius Solis* sailed back to me, trailing its impaled cargo behind. I caught it and shook the pumpkin carcass off with a flourish. The juice sizzled off the surface of the blade. It smelled vaguely roasted and rotten.

"Show off," he said affectionately. "You get points for style and points for precision, but that's it."

I sauntered in closer. "What about points for being a badass, sexy Wonder Woman?" The sword went back to my belt.

Deacon grabbed my waist. "None of that makes you a better shot," he said.

I put my hand over my heart and pretended he'd wounded me. "Ouch. And they say romance is dead."

"Truth hurts, beautiful. I don't make the rules." He chuckled and leaned down to touch his forehead to mine. I wrapped my arms around his neck and lifted onto my toes. Our lips were inches apart when the coarse squawk of the radio on my chest killed the mood.

"Hey, guys." Luis's voice crackled over the channel. "You gotta get back in here—like, right now."

I pulled away from Deacon and thumbed the button. "Now?" I repeated. "What's wrong?"

"Nothing's wrong," the kid replied. "Your friends from DC are here. They want to spill the beans."

Deacon and I looked at each other and set off for the main building. I took Marcus's medallion from my pocket and slipped the chain over my head. "Roger that," I told Luis. "We're on our way."

## CHAPTER TWO

Deacon and I were the last to arrive at the fort's only real conference area. Everyone else had already grouped around the long, glossy table. I shut the door as we entered and made a mental tally of faces. Steph and Frank stood amid the usual suspects and I couldn't help but notice how closely they'd positioned themselves.

Then I had to do a double-take at Frank because damn, the man looked great. He was still not my type, but he was now a far cry from the corpulent, downtrodden gangster I had once loved to hate. He'd trimmed down a ton, and without the dead weight and the dark circles, there was a certain silver-screen charm about his rough features.

"Steph." Deacon moved forward and enveloped his ex-partner in a hug. "It's as good as hell to see you."

She gave him a half smile. "And you, St. Clare. I hope you weren't worried. You of all people know how hard it is to get rid of me." They shared a chuckle. Over Steph's shoulder, Frank caught my eye and I had to pretend I hadn't stared at him.

He grinned. "Did ya miss me, Vic? By the look on your face, I'd almost think you were happy to see me."

"Don't read too much into it, Frank," I said. "I'm only glad you're back in off the streets."

Shortly thereafter, I called the meeting to order. "Let's get this ball rolling. We have a lot of information to exchange."

"How were things out west?" Steph asked. "We received snippets from Maya, but not too much. DC is a disaster. It's difficult to get communications in or out."

I drummed my fingers on the tabletop and glanced at the circle of faces. "Well, we flew out, we killed some gods, and we found Delano."

"No shit?" Frank asked. He frowned almost regretfully. "We caught wind of his name a few times too. I haven't seen that son of a bitch since..." He made a general motion at his vampy appearance. "You know."

"It turns out he's been pretty freaking busy," I said. "The dude's on a rampage, killing gods and absorbing their powers. He's becoming some kind of bizarre amalgamation of every god he's managed to defeat." I recalled the image of Delano's long black hair turning gold as Oxylem's lifeless body drifted away on the tide.

"I didn't know that was possible," Maya said. "Does it hurt him at all?"

I shook my head. "I wish, but it's the other way around. He gets stronger every time he does it."

Steph piped up again. "But you still kicked his ass, right?"

"We didn't fight," I said. "I don't think he wanted to, for

whatever reason. He arrived, then screwed off, and we came back here."

"Damn," she said. "He sounds like a guy who could use a good thrashing."

"Speaking of screwin' off, where the hell is Brax?" Frank asked and swiveled his head to look around the room.

"Yeah." I snuck a look at Jules, who refused to return it. "He's in the wind as usual. He split right after we touched down on the east coast. Said he had something he needed to do, but I sure as hell don't know what that is."

*Perhaps it is for the best that the demon remains absent,* Marcus suggested. *He may be somewhat reformed, but I maintain that his most prevalent talent is to attract trouble of all kinds.*

I laughed. "Somewhat reformed? That's all you can give him?"

*It is all he has earned.*

"You might be right," I said. "Who needs a bullheaded, ornery old guy around when we've already got you? I'm beginning to think that the real reason you don't like Brax is because you're too much alike."

*This is slanderous language,* the centurion warned grumpily.

"Oh, please," I said. "Brax earns his keep. We all know it. Sometimes, I really can't believe how stubborn you are."

Deacon nodded. "I'll admit that he can be pretty weird, but if there's anything I've learned about Brax by now, it's that he'll turn up when he's good and ready. Say whatever you want about him, he always does."

A murmur of general agreement ran through the room.

Jules had graduated to making eye contact with me, but her face remained impassive. She had yet to open up about what was going on between her and the demon, but I was her best friend and I had my theories.

I turned back to Steph and Frank. "Tell me about the capital," I said. "On a scale of 'not at all' to 'totally,' how fucked is it?"

She considered my rating system. "It's seriously fucked," she said finally. "But not hopeless. The city's overrun, for sure, with a bunch of gods and other stuff. None of them have a solid presence like they did in New York, though." She looked at Frank. "What do you think?"

The former mobster pulled a face. "It ain't a pretty sight," he admitted. "I can't say one way or the other if there's much left worth fighting over. It looked like it wasn't anything more than a free for all from where we stood." He paused. "Except that one place."

Steph nodded. "True. There's one area between the Washington Monument and the Lincoln Memorial that appeared to have been secured against the Forgotten. We didn't get close enough to infiltrate, but we could see human troops patrolling a fairly wide perimeter, particularly around Lincoln. They were trying to clear out more so they could expand."

"And weren't doing a half-bad job, neither," Frank added. "By the time we left, they gained some ground."

She folded her arms. "Of course, we almost didn't get to leave at all, what with this clumsy lunk picking fights over territory." Although she glared daggers at Frank, her mouth held the hint of a smile.

"Hey!" he retorted, instantly on the defensive. "Did you

want a closer look or not, woman? I can tell you from experience, these guys are beasts. The only rules they know are pack rules, and that means you fight for dominance."

"You nearly had your ass kicked for dominance," she said. "Just saying."

Frank puffed up indignantly. "I had to make it believable," he said. "I coulda beat the living daylights out of all of them, but do you think we would've gone undercover after that? No, sir."

She glanced meaningfully at me. "He almost had his rear end handed to him on a silver platter. Don't ask me how he pulled it off in the end." She rolled her eyes. "Oh, wait, I saved his knuckleheaded ass." She flashed Frank a real smile as she said that.

He grinned back. "Only a little. I had it covered for the most part."

Steph patted his back. "Whatever helps you sleep at night, champ."

I observed the exchange in stunned silence, barely comprehending what I saw. What the hell was going on there? How much weird subtext had I missed? I shook my head slightly. At least Deacon and I somewhat made sense together.

Frank cleared his throat. "Don't listen to the lady, Vic. I got in far enough to see something interesting, which is that someone's set up shop in the memorial. They cut Lincoln's head off and everything. Ballsy move, if you ask me."

"You'll never guess who it was," Steph interjected. She looked at Deacon. "Our old friend."

Deacon blinked. "You're kidding."

"Nope. We found him there, doing what he does best." She mimed the act of smoking a cigarette, and I realized she was talking about the man from Central Park who'd shown up at the tunnel out of New York City.

"He cut Lincoln's head off?" I asked, dumbfounded.

She shrugged. "It might not have been him who did that. But I wouldn't be too surprised if it was, honestly." She stopped fake smoking. "He said he wants to see you, by the way. As soon as possible. He said it was urgent."

I ran my hand through my hair. "Of course." A feeling I couldn't quite explain wormed its way down into my stomach—like doubt mixed with resignation. Ordinarily, my gut might have advised me not to trust a person who possibly committed acts of vandalism on a national monument. But at the same time, it was impossible to pretend that the mysterious man hadn't come through for me on multiple occasions.

Besides that, as usual, what choice did we have? One way or another, Delano had to be stopped. I already knew we'd need all the allies we could get.

"Well," I said. "I know what we're doing tomorrow. Next stop, DC."

# CHAPTER THREE

I had slowly adjusted to being up at the crack of dawn
and now trudged toward the trucks in the early, pale
grey light. This time, I had everyone but Dan, Veronica,
Jules, and Luis. The kid had begged me, practically on his
knees, to ship out with the rest of us, but I'd played the bad
cop and told him he had to stay. "Dan needs a righthand
man," was what I told him. Luis was plainly less than
convinced, but his admirable sense of duty finally won out
and he returned to the fort without a continued fight.

After that, the goodbyes were brief. We loaded into the
trucks and drove out to the road in less than ten minutes.
The way to the interstate was cold and dusty and the big
wheels kicked up dirt and frost as we tracked our way to
the highway. "You just got back and I've made you retrace
your steps," I said apologetically to Frank. "Sorry about
that."

He sat in the passenger seat with his elbow on the
window sill and stared directly ahead out the windshield.

"Don't worry about it," he said. "It's all in a day's work. And it beats sitting around on my ass doing nothing."

On that much, we agreed. "Tell me about it," I said. I glanced constantly in the rearview mirror, even though the road was eerily empty, and marveled at the changes that had taken place in Frank. "You know, you look awesome," I told him. "You're, like, glowing."

"I ain't knocked up if that's what you're getting at," he said gruffly.

We both laughed. "Getting out on the road has been good for you," I told him. "I don't think I've ever seen you this happy."

The vampire mumbled something unintelligible and turned his face away. I thought I caught a glimpse of a blush creeping into his cheeks. "I don't know what you're talking about," he managed awkwardly and stared fixedly out the window. A few moments of silence passed. "I guess I never thought the apocalypse would be the thing to change my life for the better."

"Oh?" I kept my voice carefully neutral. "I thought this had something to do with a certain blonde FBI bombshell."

The blush intensified to the point where it became impossible to hide. Frank hemmed and hawed for a while, clearly uncomfortable with the line of questioning, but I could also tell he wanted to talk about it, at least a little. "It's nothing," he said after a protracted pause. "We just…" He trailed off and shrugged his broad shoulders.

"Just what?" I prodded like an annoying sibling or a nosy friend. "Just really like each other? Just want to get married and have a picket fence, two and a half kids, and a family dog?"

The ex-mobster gave me a warning look. "I don't know about any of that half a kid bullshit, but…" He exhaled a big breath. "I don't know, all right? We mighta hooked up once or twice. Or a few times."

I smiled triumphantly. "There it is."

"What can I say?" He threw his hands up. "It's been a helluva long time since I had anyone to care about. Longer than that since anyone cared about me. I'd be lying if I said it didn't feel real nice."

*I do not support this union,* Marcus complained. *Such fraternizing between a human and a Forgotten is no less than an abomination. It is surely an ill omen.*

I shushed him hard with my mind, unwilling to dampen Frank's newfound serenity in any way. He might have been a lowlife thug when we first met, but the guy was on the up and up, and I liked him. The least he deserved was a chance.

"Did she make you sleep on the couch after she had to rescue you from that fight?" I asked, mostly joking.

He chuckled. "She threatened, but nah. She's not that scary when you get down to it. I mean, not *it.*" The blush returned with a vengeance. He struggled to find more appropriate phrasing. "She's a good cop. Found out a lot of stuff. She wanted to go farther in instead of me when we reached the Memorial, but I told her a human approaching would be too suspicious. They coulda shot her on sight." He scratched his chin. "I pretended to be a regular vamp and bellied up to the perimeter. I let 'em fight me off, but not before I had a good look at the place."

I opened my mouth to ask for more details. Instead, a curse emerged. "Shit!" I grabbed the wheel with both hands and stomped the brake. The truck went into a sideways skid and sprayed dust and gravel up against the body. As the cloud cleared, Frank and I stared at a watery chasm framed by two ragged segments of what had once been a bridge.

"What the fuck?" Frank muttered.

"It looks like it's out," I said.

The vamp shook his head. "This can't be right. It wasn't out yesterday."

I raised an eyebrow. "Are you sure?"

"It couldn't have been out," he insisted. "We crossed it on our way to the fort."

A car door slammed behind us. Moments later, Deacon walked past my window. He inspected the stub of the bridge in front of the truck before he returned and tapped on the glass. I rolled it down.

"I'm not an expert, but I think this was done on purpose," he said. We looked at each other and obviously shared the same thought.

I threw open my door and hollered, "Ambush!"

The other vehicles pulled in tight and we gathered in the center, circled, and faced outward. The thick trees on either side of the road quivered with hellish, unearthly growls.

"You could've told us you had planned a family reunion, Maya," Steph joked.

"Call it a surprise party," she shot back. "I have to admit, they almost got me." She hulked out as a wave of mangy fur and glistening fangs exploded through the tree line. The howls were enough to rattle my teeth. I clenched my jaw and drew my sword.

Deacon and Steph opened fire first. On my right, Frank charged the nearest werewolf and instantly tore out a huge chunk of the creature's throat. The wolf staggered, reverted to human form, and clutched at the wound. Before it even hit the ground, the vampire leapt onto his next victim. He was astonishingly fast now, much like the vamps I'd fought in the slaughterhouse, and he still impacted like a semi.

I dodged the Were with the missing trachea and struck out at the legs of the one right behind it to bring the beast to its knees. On instinct, I planted the *Gladius Solis* into the hard, half-frozen ground and used my momentum to swing around. The blade came free as I sailed forward and lopped the wolf's head cleanly off its neck on my way past. The feverish yellow eyes glazed over, and the body slumped heavily. I hit the ground running and thrust the sword into a Were's chest. The bones stood out in sharp, emaciated relief beneath its shoddy hide.

"I thought these fleabags were on our side!" Frank yelled. He swung from side to side as he clung tenaciously to the unkempt scruff of a large Were's neck. Before it could shake him off, three bullets perforated its skull in quick succession. The vampire rode the corpse to the ground.

"You're welcome," Steph called. "Again." She turned and delivered a roundhouse kick into the ribcage of a Were poised to leap. It crumpled and she stepped on its neck.

"Hell of a woman," Frank said. He dusted his hands off. "Like I was saying, I thought they were with us."

"Some of them are." I parried a claw strike with my blade, which proceeded to melt the creature's claws to

21

stubs. "Not all of them. The ones in Washington—" I paused to grapple the Were, threw him backward, and pinned him with the sword. "The ones in Washington didn't spend that much time with the god who turned them. I had the chance to revise their conditioning, so to speak. There's no helping these guys. They're starving and feral."

They didn't even appear to have retained the ability to speak in anything but beastly noises. Every last shred of humanity in their eyes was long gone. It was a wonder they could even take the bridge out or plan this ambush. And yet, there we were.

*Most of the creatures produced as Forgotten have no sense of humanity at all,* Marcus said. *They cannot be grouped with the likes of their former brethren, no matter where their origins lie. Individuals such as Maya and Frank must be viewed as the exception, rather than the rule.* He said the last part stiffly like he was frowning.

I looked into the sea of frothing Weres and for once, I was tempted to simply agree. "Why do they always have to travel in packs?" I asked out loud.

As if in answer, three bullet holes materialized neatly in the three nearest beasts, directly between their blazing eyes. "They know I need target practice," Steph said. She dropped three more in the span of a few seconds.

"See, Vic?" Deacon asked. "That could be you, but you keep playing."

I glowered at him. The *Gladius Solis* flew from my hand, plunged through an oncoming Were, out his back, and through the neck of the one behind him. I didn't flinch as it returned smoothly into my hand.

"Does it look like I'm playing?" I demanded.

"Holy shit," Steph said. She nodded over my shoulder, and I turned in time to see Maya break a Were's back, toss the limp corpse onto a pile of others, throw her head back, and howl her dominance. She grabbed the last of her challengers by the chest fur, slammed the wolf into the ground, and used her weight and strength to crush its considerably frailer frame. She snapped its neck in one swift movement. The sharp crack of bone resounded in the sudden silence.

"They're leaving!" Deacon announced. "Looks like they're not so dumb after all." The few survivors of the horde had turned tail and loped into the dark recesses of the forest, leaving a trail of their dead. We regrouped at the cars and Maya threw on a spare change of clothes.

"Nice job, team," I said. "We kicked all kinds of werewolf ass. And now, the million-dollar question is how the hell do we get ourselves across the river?"

## CHAPTER FOUR

Our quest to ford the river took us miles downstream, where we found a spot we could get across with only mild panic in our chests. The water surged almost to the hoods of our trucks at times, but we made it to the opposite bank, up the incline, and back toward the nearest road.

Frank and I spent a lot of the drive catching up, and when we were through with that, we drove in companionable silence. Occasionally, we scanned for radio stations, and we always kept our eyes peeled for more trouble. Deacon and I exchanged status reports between trucks every hour or so. Outside the windows, the ravaged landscape rolled by.

There wasn't much to see aside from ruined farmland and old, splintery barns, so the sight of a ramshackle diner on the side of the road caught all our attention. We pulled into the unpaved lot with the intention to search the place for any leftover food. As I killed the engine, I noticed that the diner's neon sign flickered and that people moved around inside. The long counter was manned, and a few booths were occupied.

"Ain't this a fine how-do-you-do," Frank remarked flatly.

"Let's hope we don't need a reservation," I said.

We joined the rest of our team and walked through the door. Nobody looked up from their meals or conversation. A haggard waitress with dark circles like moon craters etched under her eyes nodded at me and gestured toward a large round table at the back.

On my way through the dining area, I examined the other patrons furtively. They all looked bone-tired and like they were covered in a fine layer of dust. The atmosphere inside the run-down establishment was one of thorough exhaustion.

We could all relate.

The crew breathed a communal sigh of relief as we settled into our seats, grateful for a few minutes out of the car to grab a bite to eat. The waitress brought us glasses of water and we skimmed the menu.

"This is weird," Maya said and broke the relative quiet. "It feels wrong."

"We saw shit like this all over the place in and around D.C.," said Frank. "Plenty on the way, too. People are starting to try to build something from their shattered lives. They want things to be normal, even if they know it's only a damn charade."

Steph nodded. "We heard that workers had returned to power plants and phone companies to try to get services up and running reliably. No one told them to. They're doing it because that's all they can do."

*It is a familiar narrative,* Marcus agreed. *For centuries, we have built civilization from the fires of hell, of war, and of disaster. Misfortune continues to befall us, worse now than ever. And yet, people remain fundamentally resilient.*

I studied our surroundings more closely. Now that we'd been seated and had started to talk among ourselves, some of the other tables had finally taken notice. Their eyes settled on me like weights but I chose to ignore them.

"The whole country must be like this," Deacon said. "We crash-landed in the Midwest for a minute on our way to Washington, and we found more Forgotten without even trying. I think it's all overrun."

Maya shuddered. "I can't even imagine three thousand miles of this," she said. "I wonder how many humans are alive out there."

"More than we fear and less than we hope," I said. "The best way to rescue them at this point is to get to the bottom of this awful mess."

She nodded. "Agreed. But I hope that doesn't take too long. Something tells me there isn't much time."

The waitress returned. We ordered our food in a somber, contemplative mood. When she left, Frank cleared his throat. "Steph suggested we stick around outside D.C. and open one of those modern bed and breakfasts. All cozy-like. Just shut out the rest of the world going to hell."

Steph burst out laughing. "That was your idea, you son of a bitch!" she exclaimed. "I think it's utterly ridiculous."

"Maybe not," he said. "I hear property taxes are lower than ever." He winked and she swatted his arm.

The mood held until our meals arrived, and we dug in and got down to business. "It ought to be easy to get into the city," Frank reassured us. "We didn't have no trouble. It took longer to fight our way out on account of them flocking toward the city centers."

"Now that New York City's more or less fallen, many of the stray Forgotten appear to be searching for a new home base," Steph explained. "Things can get fairly hairy."

Frank waved the possibility away. "It'll be fine," he said. "We're as tough as nails. We can do this."

"I've heard that one before," Deacon remarked grimly. "What could go wrong?"

Frank stuck the last bite of food from his plate into his mouth, chewed quickly, and swallowed. "Here's what I'm not a hundred percent sold on," he said. "How do we know we can really trust this guy—the smoking jackass, or whatever you call him? Does anybody have any dirt we can use?"

All eyes turned to Deacon. He took a swig of his water. "Look, I don't know much," he said cautiously. "Definitely not much more than Steph. The guy's a damn ghost. He showed up one day early on, dropped some intel, and disappeared. A short while after, he showed up again, dropped some more, and disappeared. It's like he leaves trails of breadcrumbs for us to follow but only he really knows where they lead. No one in the Bureau that I could talk to knew a single thing about where he came from. That's all we have."

Frank scoffed. "It sounds shady to me," he grumbled.

I stretched and leaned back in my chair. The patrons at the table behind us huddled close together and whispered among themselves. A few phrases caught my nectar-heightened ears.

"I think that guy is one of them. Look at his skin."

"Did you see his eyes? Why are his clothes all torn up like that?"

"Why don't *her* clothes fit? Those freaks must be hiding something."

The blood boiled hot into my face and tinged my vision red. I clenched my fists, about to teach those nosy pricks exactly how to mind their own business. As I moved to push my chair out, Marcus spoke.

*Do not act on rash emotions, Victoria. I understand that their words are ignorant and hurtful, but it is only natural for humans to despise a being like Frank—and Maya, if they truly knew her nature. This is the way of things. Indeed, these instincts have kept many a human alive in dire times.*

I bit my lip so hard I tasted blood and willed my head to cool. The desire to knock someone's block off still burned within me, but I tried to be sensible instead. Starting a fight would hardly make things easier for us now. The very last thing we needed was unwanted attention.

"Okay, guys," I announced and shoved my chair back. "It's time for us to get back on the road."

Deacon glanced at me but didn't question my decision. We left money for our bill on the counter and I led our crew the hell out of there. Back in the truck cab, I hazarded a glance through the front window of the diner. The patrons in the booth behind us stared at me with raw animosity in their eyes.

The hair on the back of my neck prickled. I jammed the key into the ignition, started the engine, and accelerated out of that place as fast as I could.

## CHAPTER FIVE

The remainder of the journey to the capital was quiet and far more tense than before. I shoved our experience at the diner to the back of my mind. Common sense told me I needed to focus on what lay ahead and what we might find as we reached the outskirts of DC. We had barely entered the official city limits when my view of the deserted road changed dramatically. I put my foot on the brake.

"Damn it," I murmured. "What the hell is going on here?"

There was no mistaking the distinctive dark green color and boxy outline of the military trucks.

Frank's fingers drummed restlessly on his knees. "Lock the doors," he said. "I don't know what they want, but they won't get it without a fight."

I sighed. "No, no, hold on. The smoking dude brought the army to Lincoln Tunnel, remember? They could be on our side. The blockade simply gave me a minor heart attack. That's all." I eased our vehicle to the front of the barricade and slowed to a stop. The vampire balled his hands into fists to keep his fingers still.

A soldier approached the door, decked out in full combat gear. He peered at me from under his helmet. "Vic Stratton?" he asked after an extended period of scrutiny.

"Yeah." My voice and demeanor remained cool. I had no idea how the strange man knew how to expect us, but decided to work with what I had until I knew more.

The soldier nodded. "We've been instructed to escort you down to the Memorial. Pull through here and follow us, please." He signaled for his compatriots to move the center of the barricade aside, which revealed an envoy of waiting transports. They flanked us as we proceeded through.

"See?" I told Frank. "Nothing to worry about."

"Right," he answered. "I'll believe it when I lay eyes on this weirdo for myself."

The escort blocked out the view from either side, but we were still treated to a dismal, head-on view of a broken city. Much as we had seen in New York, heaps of rubble and debris lined the streets and blocked some of them off entirely. Several small fires burned along the roadside, which was also crowded with the usual mess of abandoned cars. Many of the buildings we passed had obviously been abandoned, looted, and vandalized, or some combination of the three. By now, I was numbed to that kind of scene. The whole damn country looked this way.

The National Mall sprawled before us and I sucked in a sharp breath. The Capitol Building towered high above our solemn parade, its dome shattered into jagged pieces. The walkways leading to the building were broken and treacherous as if an earthquake had ripped through. Barely over a mile down the Mall, the Washington Monument leaned dismally. It had been broken and now stabbed into the grass at its base. Huge cracks riddled the stonework and radiated through the ground at the site of impact.

"What a fucking mess," I said quietly. "I wonder which royal jackass is responsible for that." Frank didn't have an answer.

Beyond the Monument, the west end of the Mall appeared incongruously normal. The Lincoln Memorial stood at the edge of the reflecting pool, regal as ever. I could barely see the looming silhouette of Honest Abe as we approached, but something wasn't quite right.

Soon, however, my attention shifted to the forces strung thickly around the edge of the Memorial grounds and all the way up the stairs. They watched us disembark from our trucks, saluted our escort, and waved us through.

"This way," said the soldier who'd greeted us at the blockade. I expected him to lead us up the steps, but instead, he moved around the side toward an inconspicuous door tucked into the base of the Memorial. I hesitated and glanced up the marble stairs. Lincoln had been beheaded and his statue ended in nothing more than a rough marble stump.

"Keep moving, please," the soldier called back. I jogged to catch up. The image of headless Lincoln lingered in my mind's eye. *Talk about an ill omen.*

Behind the plain door, we were met by yet another guard, who took one look at us and held his hand up. "Hold it," he said brusquely and stared at Frank. "He can't come any farther."

I bristled. "Why not?" The edge in my voice couldn't be concealed. I might have expected this kind of ignorance from laypeople, maybe, not someone with the smoking man's obvious authority.

The guard frowned at me. He was blunt in his reply. "Because he's a vamp. There's a strict no-monster policy here." He paused to let the words sink in and then repeated himself. "He can't come any farther. He'll have to stay outside."

"Are you kidding me?" I asked and gritted my teeth. "This is fucked." For the second time that day, blood rushed to my head.

Maya placed her hand on my shoulder. "Vic," she said soothingly. "It's fine. Frank and I can wait outside. Right, Frank?"

The vampire's gaze bounced quickly between me, Maya, and the guard. "Uh, sure," he said and shuffled backward. "Go on without us, boss. We'll wait here."

The guard glanced curiously at Maya. "Only him, honey," he told her. "You can come on in."

She smiled sweetly. "No, I can't. I'm afraid it would be against your policy." His eyes widened and he studied her with futile interest. She held the smile on her face. "Let's say that Frank, here, is a daydream. I'm your worst nightmare."

The guard swallowed. He beckoned the rest of us onward as Maya and Frank retreated into the daylight. I brushed past him harder than necessary.

*Although Maya is but little, she is fierce,* Marcus commented.

"She's not always that little, either," I said.

We passed into the halls of a tiny museum dedicated to the sixteenth president, which featured a wall of plaques and an austere portrait of his face on one wall. The space had otherwise been converted into an open office. Everything was polished to an absurd shine. Pieces of furniture softened the place, including a large, dark wood desk situated in front of a wall of matching bookshelves. The smoking man stood between desk and shelves and white plumes billowed from his lips. He looked immaculate.

When he saw us, he smiled. "Welcome, Vic. Please, do your best to make yourselves at home. I am pleased to see you've taken my advice to heart and collected a fine company of warriors."

"It'd be even finer if you hadn't forced me to leave my best one at the door," I said. Frustration bubbled immediately below the surface. Maya had spent months at my side. I resented that she wasn't allowed to be there now.

"A shame," he agreed. "But it can't be helped. Your friends have proven their worth, but their nature leaves something to be desired. Trusting the Forgotten is all but impossible."

I scowled. "That's a pretty messed up thing to say. You don't make much of a case for yourself here." Everyone wanted to walk on thin ice today. I resisted the mighty urge to crack my knuckles.

Deacon cleared his throat. "You asked for us, sir," he said. "We're here. Tell us what's going on."

The smoking man took a long drag on his cigarette. His gaze roamed each of our faces. "Delano's location has been pinpointed," he began. "He's in the Midwest—essentially, the middle of nowhere. Nothing but flat, out-of-season cornfields as far as the eye can see." He puffed again. "A perfect place to raise a massive army and especially if the lesser gods—of which the number is increasing—continue to bow at his feet. I suspect that soon, he will have found a way to force the stronger ones into line as well. Our task is to stop him before that happens."

My ears perked up, albeit grudgingly. "Or else what?"

He turned his calm, impassive eyes to me. "Or else the human world ends," he said simply. "Delano is the biggest threat we know, bar none. Up until now, uncontrolled chaos between the gods has allowed some space for those humans who have survived to run, to hide, and to fight. If Delano is able to bring about some semblance of unity, even if he must do so by force, there will be nowhere for mankind to go. The truth is as stark and cruel as that."

"Awesome," I said flatly. "What's the bad news?"

The smoking man smiled. "Provided that we are able to defeat Delano, the other gods will then fear us in his stead. They will flee or be banished. We can take this nation back, and from here, the rest of the Earth." He flicked the ash carelessly from his cigarette. "As far as strategy is concerned, I have contacts within the uncompromised sectors of the United States Military resistance. They are standing by to coordinate a strike with you and your team, should you choose to do so."

For a moment, we simply stared at one another. "We have to confer," I said finally.

"Of course." The man turned his back. "I need not remind you that time is a luxury."

Deacon, Steph, and I snapped into a quick huddle. I looked at them and wished the other two-fifths of my team had been permitted to join us. "It's a huge risk," I said. "We don't have any idea how strong Delano is now, and I'm a hundred percent positive that he will expect an attack. There's no way we'd be able to catch him by surprise."

"Also, I'm kind of with Frank on this guy," Steph said, her voice low. "He made us leave our brawlers at the door because he says we can't trust them? I don't think so. He's the one we shouldn't trust. We don't know anything about him."

"He hasn't steered us wrong yet, Steph," Deacon said. "It's not like we have a folder full of fallback plans. This is now down to the wire. There's no room to second-guess anything here."

"The whole world is at stake," she fired back. "Not only the free one. Everything. Second-guessing seems like the smartest thing we can do." She turned to me. "I don't like it, Vic."

"And I don't think it matters whether we like it or not," Deacon said. "It's this or nothing."

*It is a quandary,* Marcus interjected. *But I can vouch for urgency in this decision. Delano is ruthless and his power only increases. If he is not unseated, all will be as the gentleman has said. I believe the best course of action is to strike for the kill.*

His voice was cut off when a soldier burst in through the entrance to the museum. "Sir!" he cried, out of breath. "We're under attack!"

## CHAPTER SIX

Our huddle broke immediately and we barreled past the guards outside to rejoin Maya and Frank. The forces on the perimeter were already engaged with a significant number of short, brutish golems.

They weren't fast, nor were they even very big, but they could pack a crazy wallop. A soldier was thrown back onto the steps from a single punch and grimaced in pain. The mirror-like surface of the reflecting pool churned, and more golems rose dripping from the water.

"Damn it to hell!" I cursed. My blade blazed into my hands and I raised it to meet the advancing ranks.

The golems proved to be relatively easy to hack apart, although they were sturdy and often continued to move as long as their legs remained intact. Without heads, they swung blindly as if in an attempt to land a crippling blow. I danced nimbly in and out of range, sliced them down, and launched heavy chunks of their crude limbs at those who still attacked. They staggered beneath the weight of their fallen comrades.

Frank wrenched a head off and heaved it into the water. Despite the weight he'd lost, he was still built like a brick shithouse, and he weathered punches and kicks like taps on the shoulder. Each time a golem was stalled by the impact of a bullet from Steph or one of the soldiers, the vampire seized it and tore into its dense, muddy flesh until it collapsed. Bodies sank into the depths of the pool they'd come from—those that stayed intact, anyway. Maya's tactic was to crush them into dust against the ground. I hoped the museum guard had a front row seat to all her werewolf glory.

Choppy waves lapped at the edge of the stone we stood on. I kicked another golem into the pool. A strange, deep rumble started low in my ears. The waves in the pool grew larger, and the earth quaked enough to catch me off guard.

"Back up!" I yelled and leapt toward the stairs. The center of the shallow pool bulged upward and exploded into a shower of water and huge chunks of rock and dirt.

I ducked and cursed as a piece of concrete landed inches to my left. When I looked up again, all the water at our side of the pool had gone and left a shallow basin with a gaping hole in the center. A craggy, two-legged behemoth straddled the hole, its entire body crusted with grimy rock. It hunched over, flexed two powerful arms, and emitted a roar.

"What the fuck is that?" someone shouted.

I rolled my eyes. Questions were for amateurs. I'd become a pro long before. "Any ideas on this chump?" I asked Marcus as I brandished the *Gladius Solis*.

*An Apprenti, for certain,* Marcus said. *A true god would*

*have stronger minions. I cannot say I know this one in particular, although I would venture to guess that his strength is his most fearsome characteristic.*

"Somehow, I'm not worried that it will think me to death," I said. The behemoth's eyes tracked instantly to the sword's fiery glow. It smiled and exposed a mouthful of sharp black teeth.

"God-killer!" it thundered. Its deep voice resonated across the Mall. "We meet at last. Your puny weapon stands no chance against the likes of me. Prepare to be slain."

"Wow," I said. "Those were more words than I assumed you knew. And here I thought you wouldn't impress me at all."

The ugly son of a bitch laughed. "Mockery is the bastion of the weak," he proclaimed and stepped out of the empty pool. The bare stone cracked beneath his feet. "It is useless within the arena of war. Either fight or die." He swept one club-like arm out and the gesture caused the soldiers around me to scatter. More little golems now surged up from the hole the behemoth had made with his grand entrance.

I nodded toward them. "Take care of the small fry. I'll handle Ben Grimm over here." The stone hulk very obviously readied himself to deliver a serious punch, but I dashed in under his arm and drove the point of my sword toward his chest with all my might.

Sparks flew on impact, but the hard plating still melted under the intense heat of the blade. I felt his thick, clumsy hands try to grip me and lift me off my feet. If he managed to get ahold of me, I might be in trouble.

I spun away and slashed at his fingers. One blocky thumb tumbled to the ground near my feet. A burning orange gash materialized across his rough palm. The Apprenti jerked his hand back and growled in pain. He lunged forward suddenly, his good hand open for a powerful blow. The rush of wind fluttered my hair as I dodged out of the way in the nick of time.

"Float like a butterfly," I said and hefted my sword into position. "Sting like a fucking bee."

Once more, I leapt into range. He threw himself forward and rained sediment down on me. His fists slammed at the place where I'd stood scant seconds before but I was too damn fast. I used his bent leg as a launching point, jumped as high as I could, and anchored the sword deep in the Apprenti's bulky shoulder. His skin began to melt into a sludgy, muddy substance.

Gravity did the rest of the work. The *Gladius Solis* slid downward through the behemoth's torso and sliced into his chest and ribs. Pieces crumbled off his body, and when my feet touched the ground, his entire right side peeled away. He teetered on one foot, only to be pelted in the face by his own minion. I looked over my shoulder and Maya grinned as she stretched her throwing arm.

The stone Apprenti toppled into the drained reflecting pool and a shockwave rippled outward from his body. The basin shattered, but the ground held it in place. I turned to face my team and the other soldiers. They all stared dumbly at me, their jaws more or less on the floor. The man himself had made his way onto the marble stairs below the entrance to the Memorial's central chamber. He was still smoking.

I strode closer through a mess of golem carnage and planted one foot on a step. "I'm tired of this shit," I told him and raised my voice so everyone could hear. "And I guess that means I'm in. Now, I'm gonna come up there, and you'll tell me how in hell we bring Delano down."

## CHAPTER SEVEN

An hour later, we were back at the trucks and preparing to leave D.C. Whatever else I could have said about the guy and his damn cigarettes, he came more prepared than most others I'd met along the way. We would return to Fort Victory with a plan, and that made our otherwise empty hands more bearable. Part of me had hoped he'd give us a secret weapon or something, but I should have known it would never be that easy.

"Vic." His voice stopped me halfway through the truck door—passenger side this time. Frank sat behind the wheel and looked ready to simply hot-foot it out of there.

I gave him an apologetic glance. "Can you hold it for, like, one second? I'll keep this as short as I can."

"Take your time," the vampire said. A drop of irony laced his next words. "It must be important."

"It had better be." I slammed the door and turned to face our host. We were all at least a little antagonized by him, and I was determined not to let him waste my time.

Sharing his strategy against Delano had only bought him provisional amnesty as far as I was concerned.

Nobody put Maya in the corner.

He didn't come closer than ten feet, and he lit a cigarette while I waited for him to tell me what he wanted. He must've smoked a whole pack of those things over the duration of our visit alone. "I think," he said and exhaled a cloud of white smoke that wreathed around his head and shoulders, "that if this works, it will change everything."

I eyed him evenly. "There's no reason it won't work," I said. "My team and I will play our part as long as you uphold your end of the bargain."

"Naturally," he replied. Another drag ended in another billow of white. The smoke seemed to hang around him a little, almost like a clinging mist. He drifted into thoughtful silence. His eyes became distant for a moment or two. "Take care to choose your soldiers carefully when you go to face him."

I chewed the inside of my lip and raised an eyebrow. "What's that supposed to mean?" He seemed determined to irritate me beyond endurance. I could feel the ice he walked on grow thinner.

"Your friends may seem loyal to you at present, and perhaps they truly are." He flicked the end of his cigarette. "But Delano has powers beyond compare, as you've no doubt seen. Can you be certain beyond a shadow of a doubt that his presence will not change their minds? At heart, they are Forgotten. They always will be."

"Who are you talking about?" I demanded. The question was unnecessary—we both knew which two he had kept in exile outside the Memorial. I merely wanted to force him to say their names and to acknowledge the way he treated individuals who professed to be his allies. He didn't take the bait and instead, regarded me through the haze of smoke.

"Listen—" I burst out. My anger pushed through my tight control and I couldn't help it. I wanted to punch some sense into him.

He held up a hand to cut me off. "Do not misunderstand my motives, young one. All I want you to do is think about it. I'm sure your friend in the medallion would agree." His two cents apparently deposited, he turned to leave.

This time, I was the one to stop him. I had no idea what to say, only the insurmountable urge to say *something*. "Who are you?" was the question my mouth seemed determined to ask. The man halted. "Really," I added as if that helped. "I didn't come here to be jerked around."

He smiled enigmatically. "Who is anyone?" he asked. "Fear not, my friend. We'll all learn who we are before the end."

That was not the answer I wanted. I threw the truck door open and climbed furiously into the seat. "Let's go," I said to Frank. "Screw this place."

"Amen." He drove around the curve of Lincoln Circle and out to the street. The escort stuck with us until we'd returned to the highway, at which point, they fell away. I watched the military envoy turn back toward the capital in the rearview mirror.

"Hey, Marcus," I said and chose my words carefully because Frank was right there and I was the one he could hear. "Was he telling the truth about you?"

He didn't reply for a while. Frank, for his part, kept his mouth shut and his eyes on the road. At last, Marcus said, *It is possible, Victoria, that in the presence of an entity such as Delano, even the strongest convictions may waver. I cannot say that I wholeheartedly disagree with his assessment.*

Residual anger smoldered in my veins, born of a loyalty I hadn't truly considered until it was thrown into question. After all this time—all this distance, everything we'd been through together—who was some cigarette-huffing old man to doubt the bonds forged in our trials by fire? I rubbed my face with the heel of my hand and told myself to brush it off and clear my mind. He was a general in the war against the gods, nothing more. I didn't have to take his word as gospel and I resolved that I wouldn't.

He was right about one thing, though. By the end, when it mattered, we'd all know who we were. And he would know what we were made of, too.

"Are you good?" Frank asked tentatively. He hazarded a glance in my direction. "Do you want I should stop the car? You look like you might hurl. Or punch the window out."

I forced myself to grin and some of the tension melted from my body. "Nah," I said. "I'm good. We've gotta go home and get ready to kick some ass."

"Your wish is my command," the vampire said and returned the grin. The truck's engine revved as he stepped on the gas.

## CHAPTER EIGHT

I rummaged through a pile of clothes on my bed in search of a matching pair of socks. Even though we'd spent a lot of time traveling lately, it somehow still felt weird to pack a bag like this—as if I were going on vacation. I tossed another shirt in along with another pair of underwear. I had no idea how many I'd need, but then again, we were essentially clueless about many things.

For one, how the hell did I think this confrontation with Delano would go? By the time we hauled ass out to Indiana, it would realistically be weeks since I'd last seen him. He could have changed in a million different ways. Even the simple thought that I had to figure that mess out made me both frustrated and anxious. I pushed the half-full bag away and plopped heavily on the edge of the mattress.

"Damn it," I said out loud and balled my hands into fists against my thighs. "I wish I'd been able to fight him back in Washington. Of course, that was the one time he bailed instead of getting down to business."

*Please do not interpret this the wrong way,* Marcus said. *However...*

I pinched the bridge of my nose. "Oh, great. Here it comes."

*I feel that perhaps it was a fortunate decision. The magnitude of Delano's new power cannot be overstated. A battle against him would likely not have ended in your favor at that point.*

I laughed grimly. "Just say it, Marcus. He would've kicked my ass."

*And laughed about it. Raucously.*

I sighed. "I fucking hate that bastard, but you're right. He's swallowed gods left and right. I think he might be more than a god now if that's even possible."

*I shudder to think that it is, and yet, he has made it so. A legion of gods inhabiting one body. I wonder. How long can he sustain an arrangement this extreme?*

"Long enough," I answered. "It barely matters anyway. I'll drag Delano to hell or die trying."

*A hero's death,* Marcus said. He chose not to elaborate. I went back to tossing things into my bag.

The sound of the door squeaking open behind me almost didn't register over the roar of my own thoughts. It wasn't until Jules parked herself on the bed that I glanced up.

"Hey," she said. "How are you?"

I made space for her. "That's a loaded question."

She began to pluck articles of clothing from the heap and folded them into neat piles on the bedspread. "I know. I wanted to check on you and make sure you haven't totally lost your mind. You always have so much to deal with compared to me."

"That's not true," I said with a look of protest. "You're like the queen of hospitality around here. People might not know it, but you're the reason they're so happy living at Fort Victory. You've made this place a home for a ton of hopeless refugees."

She smiled slightly. "Things are never hopeless when you're around, Vic. And I'm glad you feel that way. I simply…" She paused with a bulky sweatshirt clutched in her hands and shook her head. "I guess *I'm* the one going crazy here. I'm bored! Isn't that insane?" Her laugh was as dry as bone. "Imagine being *bored* in your safehouse in the middle of the damned apocalypse. But that's the situation. Lately, I feel I could climb the walls. I can't get out of my head."

"Yeah, I've been there." I scanned my attempt to pack, decided it would have to do, and zipped the duffel bag.

"You got out of it," Jules said.

"By shipping out to Washington and almost getting killed by Vikings," I reminded her. "My solutions aren't for everyone."

She was quiet for a minute and her fingers fretted at the hem of the sweatshirt. The gears of her nimble mind worked visibly behind her eyes. "I want to go with you this time," she declared suddenly.

I was so caught off guard that I laughed, which I immediately saw was the wrong reaction. "Sorry," I said quickly. "But what are you talking about, Jules? You have zero combat training and no offense, but I've seen you shoot a gun."

She pursed her lips. "And I've seen Deacon trying to teach you."

"Hey!" I laughed and threw a shirt gently at her. "It's different for me because I have the sword. Teaching me to shoot was all Deacon's idea." I narrowed my eyes at her. "When did you watch us, anyway? He always insists that we practice alone, or else I might kill someone by accident."

My best friend smirked knowingly. "Oh, I'm so sure that's the real reason. Although it is a valid concern." Her smile faded. "I'm really happy that's working out for you two. Deacon's a great guy."

"Yeah, you look super happy." I sat down beside her. "What's up?" She shrugged and a light clicked on in my head. "Hold on a second. This is about Brax, isn't it?"

I could tell by the look on her face that I'd hit the nail on the head. She flushed pink all the way to her ears.

"I hate to break it to you," I said and nudged her in the ribs. "But it's fairly obvious."

Jules groaned. "Okay, okay. Yes, it has something to do with him. And no, I didn't expect things to turn out this way." She paused. "It's hard to admit now, but I was afraid of him at first. I thought there was no way he could ever get along with humans in a non-violent way."

I arched my eyebrows. "To be honest, I doubt even he would blame you for thinking that. Hell, until recently, he probably would've agreed with you."

She shrugged. "I know. Maybe I wanted to help him more than anything—at least in the beginning." She twirled a lock of her golden hair around her fingers. "Now, we have such a strong connection. He told me about his past, and it helped me see him in a totally different light." She looked at me with a mixture of worry and excitement in her eyes. "I'm...sort of falling for him."

I chuckled. "That seems like an understatement."

"He's my type, too, which is strange to say out loud." Her blush returned. "Rough around the edges but secretly soft-hearted. It's like he's from a romance novel. And I have to admit, I love it."

"What kind of romance novels have you read?" I teased.

Jules winked. "The good kind." She finally finished folding the sweatshirt and set it aside. "Anyway, now you know why I have to get out of here for a while. Not forever. I merely need to clear my head and get some distance so I can think about things rationally again."

I put my arm around her shoulders. "I'll let you come with us on one condition."

"Name it," she said quickly.

"You'll not fight," I told her. "You're the brains of this operation. It'd be way too dangerous to throw you into combat this late in the game without serious training. Delano's not like the chumps we fought in New York."

Jules nodded. "Don't worry, Vic. I'll take care of myself and stay out of your way."

"And you won't fight." I prodded her for verbal confirmation. Jules looked soft on the outside, but I knew better than anyone how tough she could be. I also knew that squaring up against a super god like Delano was not in her wheelhouse, regardless of how she felt about a certain demon.

She nodded again, more insistently this time. "Thank you for trusting me on this. I'll be fine. I promise." She gave me a squeeze, stood, and was out the door before I had the chance to say anything else. I stared after her.

*Victoria, I fear a mistake has been made,* Marcus said. I cringed. I had forgotten the old geezer was there. *The battlefield is no place for a woman like that. She belongs—*

"No way," I interrupted. "Don't start on where Jules belongs." I grabbed my bag, glanced down at it, and unzipped it to check its contents one last time. "Sometimes, you say stuff like that and your age really shows, dude. You have to get with the progressive picture." Satisfied with my loadout, I placed the bag by the door. "Besides, you never expected me to be this type of woman either."

*The difference is that I was able to train you first.*

"And that's why I told her she couldn't fight." I shrugged. "I'm not sure if she actually listened, but I meant what I said. I'm not above tackling her to the ground if I see her even try to pack heat."

*On the contrary, that seems a reasonable course of action for her to take. The middle of this country is cold at this time of year.*

I rolled my eyes. "I'm beginning to think you're doing this on purpose."

*Well, I am beginning to think that your trust in your friends may run too deep.*

I stopped on my way into the bathroom and caught a glimpse of my own surprise in the tiny mirror. "Whoa," I said. "Way to bring down the vibe, old man."

He didn't respond as I washed my face, brushed my teeth, and ran a comb through hair that had grown way too long. But his silence wasn't empty. I could sense his need to speak his mind.

"Come on, Marcus," I said finally. "Spill it. I have no choice but to listen to you anyway."

*You will be angry with me.*

"I might," I said. "But we'll work it out. We're both adults here."

*Very well. It is my belief that the man at the marble house was correct in his caution regarding certain members of our party.*

"Feel free to explain," I said evenly and stared hard at my reflection.

*There is no denying that Delano's strength has exceeded all previously known levels, as we have said multiple times. We know for certain that his behavior has escalated to the point where he now consumes gods entirely, and yet, there have apparently been no ill effects. Given these circumstances, it seems utterly foolish to assume that he would not be capable of controlling Frank and Maya at a moment's notice. They may be strong, but they cannot compare with entities over which Delano has already asserted his dominance.*

I took a deep breath and reminded myself not to be annoyed. This was merely typical Marcus logic as usual. "Maya was able to break away from Lupres," I said. "Frank defied Delano's orders once. He can do it again."

*Lupres cannot compare. Nor can any previous form that Delano has taken. He has transcended all boundaries. The rules by which we once were guided have lost their relevance.*

I closed my eyes and soaked his words in. They made me uncomfortable. "Speaking of which, let's talk strategy," I said briskly and snapped my eyes open. "You have advice for everything, and I'm asking for it. Tell me what my expectations should be."

This kind of thing was what Marcus was best at, and I wanted to steer him away from the doom and gloom. We needed to come at this from an optimistic place.

My plan didn't work.

*I do not know. I have been around for thousands of years. I have watched civilizations grow and die. I assumed I had seen everything and that nothing new remained. I was wrong.*

"What's the prognosis, Doc?" I asked. "Give it to me straight. I can handle it."

*The chances of victory are slim. At best.*

A knock at the door punctuated his last sentence. I stepped out of the bathroom and answered it, if only to grant myself a distraction. Deacon stood in the hall and his expression sobered as soon as he saw me.

"What's with the face?" he asked. "We haven't even left yet."

I stood aside so he could enter the room. "Oh, you know. Marcus was telling me how screwed we are."

*That is not an entirely accurate translation.*

"Since when have you ever listened to him?" Deacon reached out and grabbed me gently by the waist. "Come on. If anyone's got this, it's you."

I smiled and leaned into his chest. "That's true. I've lived on shitty odds ever since I asked Tommy Reynolds to the Sadie Hawkins Dance in high school."

Deacon snorted. "What did he say?"

I laughed. "He said no."

He kissed me on the forehead. "When this is all over, I'll find Tommy Reynolds and tell him he's a damn fool."

# CHAPTER NINE

The driver's seat of the sturdy old truck had begun to feel like a second home. I stared out at yet another empty stretch of highway as we headed west on Interstate 76. Instead of Frank, I'd opted for Deacon as my copilot, and so far, we had focused mostly on what flashed by outside the windows.

Aside from our brief touchdown mid-flight to Washington, this was our first real foray into the interior of the country. My hands on the wheel were a little tense, and I swiveled my head constantly in response to the tension I felt.

So far, the signs hadn't been very promising. The ongoing war had left its mark everywhere, even on the road. We skirted huge craters, downed trees, and piles of burned-out cars that stretched for miles. Once the forests gave way to farm country, blood was visible, splashed all across the barren, snowy fields. There were occasional bodies, too, most of them frozen like grotesque mannequins.

Deacon scrubbed a hand down his face. "It's been months, but sometimes, it still hits me real hard that this is the world now." We passed a spray of abandoned belongings scattered in a ditch off the shoulder. The blank eyes of a dirty stuffed animal watched us pass. "Shit like that makes me wonder if we'll ever see normal again."

"I think we'll get there," I said. "It won't be easy. And it probably won't look the way it did before, but that's fine. Marcus has seen a hundred different versions of normal over the course of his existence. If things go our way, he'll see hundreds more."

"That's a decent outlook," he conceded. "It doesn't really do much for us in the here and now, though." He gazed out the window at the devastated landscape. The exposed joists of a huge, ruined barn protruded into the sky. "I like to think there'll be a place and time for us to settle down."

I nodded. "There will be. I can't tell you that we'll have the neat little suburban house with the picket fence and the tree in the backyard, but we'll have something. And that it will be enough."

He squeezed my hand. "The thought of you in the suburbs is terrifying. Curlers in your hair, driving a mini-van…no thanks."

I grinned at him. "I figured that's what you would envision, Mr. Hopeless Romantic."

"I'm romantic," Deacon said. "I'm not delusional."

"Good to know." I took my left hand off the wheel and waggled my fingers at him. "You'll still get me some ice, though, right? I mean, someone ought to try to make an honest woman out of me."

He raised an eyebrow and smirked. "Did you just say 'ice?' Maybe you're more suburban than I thought."

I laughed. "Would you prefer I say 'bling?'"

He made a face. "Ugh, no. Christ, did you get your slang from Marcus?"

"No," I said. "Why?"

Deacon smiled and shook his head. "Because it's as ancient as fuck."

Three hours into the drive, my eye caught sight of a distinctive black column of smoke that rose ahead of us and off to the right. Large, birdlike shapes circled high above it and dove in and out of the plume.

"I don't like that," I muttered.

"We should check it out."

I radioed our intentions to the vehicle behind us and took the next exit off the interstate, which appeared to lead directly toward the base of the swirling smoke. As we cruised down the ramp, the flying shapes came into better focus and I realized they weren't birds at all. They were harpies.

"Shit, we have a situation here," I said. Immediately beyond the ramp, the streets were clogged with cars. Many of them were scorched and charred as usual, but a fair number were also crushed—from the top, not the front or back. Most of their windows had been blown out, and safety glass glittered over the streets.

I swerved and weaved through the mechanical carnage as we followed the signs to the outskirts of a small town—population just over a thousand. On the main street, the vehicles had been shoved unceremoniously to the side and formed a barrier of tires and smashed metal. The source of the black smoke we'd seen from the highway turned out to be buildings, including the town hall and the post office. Harpy screeches rattled the truck's windows.

"Holy shit." Deacon sat up abruptly and focused on something that lumbered from the wreckage of a residential building straight ahead. "Look at that big motherfucker."

The creature straightened and shook debris from its shoulders. Rough, leathery skin stretched over heavy muscles. The long blade of a mean-looking machete glinted in its left hand and a misshapen club dangled from its right.

"Marcus and I saw a guy like that, way back when," I said. "But he was simply fat. This one looks like he's lived off protein shakes and steroids." The ogre hefted its club across its massive shoulders and provided me a daunting display of biceps that were bigger than my head. "This will be a fun little side trip." I pressed the button on my radio. "Hey, guys. When we stop, get out and fight. We can't leave this place without clearing it."

"Roger," Maya answered. "Man, these things are ugly."

We noticed more of them as we drove a little farther. They appeared to hunt through the structures that were left and literally broke through walls with their weapons and fists. One of them yanked a struggling human from a second-story window.

"Hell no!" I declared and accelerated sharply. "Who the fuck is running this shit show? He's about to have some special guests."

The main street led to a square near the center of the town. Obviously, it had been well maintained at one time, but it was in complete shambles now. The cobblestones were crushed and trodden in, which rendered the area little more than a broken, unstable pit. In the middle of this mess stood a super-ogre, two or three times the size of the others, naked to the waist, and enormously muscular. He wore a giant smile on his ugly face as he surveyed his new, wrecked dominion.

I parked the truck at the edge of the crumbling road. Into the radio, I said, "Time to crash this wild party." After a deep breath, I opened my door and jumped out.

The sound of the truck doors slamming shut drew the large ogre's attention. His toothy smile only intensified at our approach. He released a great, belched laugh. "Who is this?" he bellowed and squinted his bloodshot eyes. "Humans too stupid to run? Surely you don't think you can stop me." We moved steadily forward and picked our way cautiously over the ground. The giant threw his head back and laughed again. "Your idiotic courage is entertaining. Never mind that I could crush each of you like gnats beneath my thumb."

I broke from the group and strode forward to crane my neck so I could look all the way up into his face. "Consider this an eviction notice," I told him. "One way or another, you'll leave today."

"Stronger warriors than you have tried to move me without success." His foul breath washed over me with every word but I stood my ground and held his gaze. "They learned quickly that I am indomitable!" He swept his hands out to encompass the square. "This is only the beginning for me. For you, it is the end."

I swung the *Gladius Solis* into view. "I beg to differ."

As soon as he felt the wash of heat from the sword's burning blade, the mega-ogre stepped back. His eyes bulged in their sockets, fixed intently on the weapon in my hands. "It's you," he said, his tone no longer grandiose. He'd rapidly become fearful and I swore I saw his hands shake. His club clattered to the ground. "The god-killer. I thought he was lying. I thought the others were cowards to run."

He took another step back.

"Sorry, pal," I said and adjusted my grip on the hilt. "I'm as real as it gets."

He threw a panicked glance over each shoulder. "Kill her!" he bellowed but his voice cracked. "Destroy the sword bearer. Now!"

Every one of his henchmen turned toward me and my comparatively tiny crew. Harpies screamed from above with claws outstretched. Maya turned faster than I'd ever seen her do it and snatched one of them out of the air to rip its wing off. The disembodied appendage was comprised of skin instead of feathers, stretched over the wing like a bat's. The Were tossed the dead harpy aside, and I noticed its body was male. Things had changed, indeed.

I turned back to the ogre god and raised my sword, only to find that he'd already bolted across the square. His heavy footfalls kicked up thick clouds of dust to mingle with the smoke. I pulled my jacket over my face and gave chase as best I could, but the small fries bogged me down. They formed a close circle around me and their eyes gleamed with malice.

"Don't worry, boys," I told them. "I'll save a dance for every one of you." The sword sizzled every time it burned through their hide. The dark, sludgy blood that spilled from the wounds smelled like a sewer. Ogre limbs rained down around me. These guys were easy, and they were simply a waste of time. I wanted their leader.

I sliced one monster cleanly in half, broke out of the circle, and raced in the direction in which I'd last seen the ogre god. A shadow fell over me and the scream of an incoming harpy tortured my ears. I readied the sword in my right hand, ready to slash backward. The sharp retort of a pistol cut the scream off and the harpy dropped to the ground at my heels.

Steph yelled, "Now you're simply showing off, St. Clare!"

I couldn't help but smile, even though I'd lost track of my quarry. The smog was too thick to see very far, and all the shrieks had made me practically deaf. I slowed, turned, and headed back toward the others. The ogre meant nothing, but I still felt the sting of disappointment in my chest. It would have been so satisfying to see that hideous head roll off into the fields.

Steph met me in the square with one foot planted atop a recently fallen foe. She took aim at a harpy and picked it out of the sky as I approached. We both tracked its descent onto the curb twenty feet away.

"Nice shot," I said.

"Tell that to Deacon," she responded with a grin. "It'll hurt more if it comes from you." She rested a hand on my shoulder. "Listen, don't stress about losing that pile of walking bullshit, all right? I've fought evil in one form or another all my life. You can't win 'em all exactly the way you want to. And sometimes, it turns out to be better that way."

"Yeah." We headed back to the vehicles together and left a trail of Forgotten corpses behind us. Maya and Frank were already there and Deacon followed close behind. I paused at the truck door and looked over the roof toward the west. "It's a good thing there's only one fight I need to win now."

## CHAPTER TEN

Deacon offered to drive for the second leg of the journey, but I declined. Being behind the wheel was comforting in a control-freak kind of way. As long as I steered the truck, I didn't feel that I barreled headlong into some bleak destiny or insurmountable obstacle. If I could steer, I could put us on a winning path.

Or so I hoped.

"Hey." Deacon's low voice intruded warmly on my thoughts. He touched his fingers to the outside of my wrist. "How are you feeling? Are you sure you don't want me to take over?"

"I'm fine," I said. "With driving, I mean."

He looked at me, both patient and expectant.

I sighed. "This is the biggest thing I've ever faced in my life," I said. "I don't know *how* I feel, except maybe that I'm standing on the edge of a cliff at the end of the world, and below me is...what? Darkness? A void? A safe place to land? There's no way to know for sure until I jump, and that's as scary as shit." I glanced at him, and he nodded.

"But at the same time, I know I can't back down. I've been called to this. It's taken a while, but I finally learned that to ignore your calling is the worst thing you can do. Especially if it involves saving all of humanity."

Deacon leaned back in his seat. "If that's the case, then I think my true calling was to be a horse trainer."

I smirked. "It sounds like you might need to find a different girl, cowboy."

He spent a good ten minutes insisting that there was a marked difference between trainers and cowboys. I remained unconvinced.

After that, we lapsed into companionable silence. I had never been the sappy, hold-hands-in-the-car sort of girl, but I did think about it once or twice. For a while, he seemed to doze.

Then he said, "Man, I hope we're ready for this."

I shot him a look. "You're the one who was all, 'no one's got this more than you,' before we left."

He scratched his chin. "Yeah, but I was talking about *you*. It's the rest of us I'm not so sure about." An undercurrent of genuine fear belied his half-joking tone.

"Relax," I said. "It'll be a piece of cake."

He pulled a face. "I don't know about that. The meeting in D.C. made it sound pretty damn hard."

I caught his eye and bit my lip. "I guarantee I've done harder. Maybe not bigger, but definitely harder."

He tried to keep his cool, but his poker face failed him. We both cracked up.

"I have to say, Vic, I'm as glad as hell to be doing this with you." He took my hand off the wheel, kissed my knuckles, and replaced it. I didn't tell him I thought he was right to wonder about our level of preparedness or even right to worry, period.

I had stared at the blank, flat line of the horizon for hours and monitored it for changes that never came. It was almost refreshing when we traversed a rare bend and saw something blocking the view. The first thing I thought was that someone had decided to build a brick wall smack in the middle of the highway. But when we moved closer, I realized there was something familiar about the texture of the material.

Crushed cars had been stacked one on top of the other, impossibly high. I could barely see the top of the metal monolith. I eased down on the brakes and marveled at the sheer scale of the thing. The truck coasted closer.

Deacon shouted, "Watch out!"

I snapped my head to the side in time to see a huge foot slam down alongside our vehicle. My foot jammed hard on the brake pedal. We screeched to a stop and stared at a giant. He was naked except for a dingy loincloth and was covered in hair from head to toe. His mile-thick skull held only one eye. Surprisingly, he didn't seem to care about the truck.

"Damn it," I muttered under my breath. I shifted the vehicle into park and unbuckled my seatbelt. "Stay put for a second. I'll handle this. I don't think it'll take very long."

"Go get 'em," he said.

I scrambled down from the cab and made my way cautiously toward the mammoth humanoid. He seemed to walk with purpose, and as I rounded the truck, I noticed his friend standing on the opposite side of the road.

The second giant gestured rudely. "What you doing,

moron?" he demanded and the words rolled out slowly. "I leave you to guard wall. You wander off. Next time I find you've walked away, I'll bash your ugly head in!"

The first giant reciprocated with an obscene gesture. His middle finger alone was almost as tall as I was and his club was actually a raw tree slung across his back. "Like to see you try," he retorted. "Road empty. No one disturb huge wall. I bored." To emphasize his point, he stamped his foot. A miniature dust storm flurried around me. "You bash my head, I kick your dick. We see who laughs then."

I coughed and brushed sediment out of my hair and off my clothes. "Hey!" I shouted. "What are you two lunkheads doing here blocking the road?"

The giant nearest to me whirled and I had to dodge the edge of his club. I leapt back as a barrage of splinters flew in my direction.

"Human!" he proclaimed and looked surprised.

The other one shambled forward. "Go back to where you came from, puny human. This area not safe for tiny things."

"We'll see about that." I whipped my sword out and lit it up. "Beat it, Andre and friend."

The giants froze. They blinked their mono-eyes at me, equal parts afraid and confused. But they didn't budge an inch. "Sorry, tiny human woman," said the first. "No can do."

"Captain's orders," added the other.

I gritted my teeth. "Fine. I warned you." With the sword held high, I moved into their range. The two gigantic creatures hesitated but raised their clubs in response.

"Hold it, you knuckle-fucks," a voice instructed from

the opposite side of the car heap. "Leave this one alone. She's with me."

We all paused and looked toward the sound. I wracked my brain in an effort to think of whom it could be. The last I'd checked, I didn't know anyone in the middle of bumfuck nowhere.

Then I saw the edge of a long black coat. Brax stepped out from the cover of the barricade with his sunglasses on and arms folded. We stared at each other, and I burst into laughter. "Oh, shit!"

"Brax!" A blonde blur tumbled out of the other truck and streaked past on my left to fly into the demon's arms. He embraced Jules with as much passion as I'd ever seen from him, and they shared a deep, intense kiss. I looked away for privacy's sake.

"Falling for him, my ass," I muttered. "You guys are balls deep."

I let them kiss it out for a minute or two before I moved in on the happy reunion. "Excuse me for breaking in on your warm and fuzzies," I said. "But what in the hell is going on?"

Brax shrugged, although he didn't release Jules. "When we got back to the fort, I received word that giants roamed around the Midwest. Two of them. Real geniuses, clearly." He glanced at the creatures who watched the whole display with mild confusion. "I knew two of these guys in Asphodel and I'd heard they got out, so I went to see if the stars had aligned. As it turns out, they had, but they were in trouble when I found them. I guess Delano's not a fan of anything bigger than he is."

"Brax helped," said a giant. "He captain now."

"I repaid a favor," the demon explained. "I killed the horde that was hunting them, and they told me Delano had a temple fortress not too far from here." He nodded toward the car monument. "I had them make that to keep anyone from getting through. They weren't kidding about it being too dangerous for humans past this point."

"Most humans," I corrected him. "That happens to be exactly where I need to go."

A grin broke out on his face. He looked at me, down at Jules, and finally at the two giants. "It looks like you're on your own for now, boys. Do the old captain a favor and carry on, all right? No one else comes through here. Humans need to be protected."

"What about that one?" the first giant asked. "And that one." He pointed at me and Jules.

Brax planted another kiss on Jules. "I've got this one," he said. He jerked his thumb at me. "That one can take care of herself. She would've thrashed the shit out of you if I let her."

They frowned and trudged away to take up posts on either side of the wall. Brax and Jules retreated to their truck, smiling like goons into each other's eyes. As I slipped behind the wheel, I heard a loud, metallic, grating sound as the giants peeled the cars apart to allow us through.

"Was that Brax?" Deacon asked. "And Jules?"

"Yep." I started the engine. "Long, weird story."

"Damn," he said. "Demons get around."

# CHAPTER ELEVEN

Almost nine hours after we left Pennsylvania, our battle caravan drove into a shadow that spread like a thick dark blanket across the Midwestern cornfields. The menacing, craggy shape of a mountain jutted from the flatlands, surrounded by absolutely nothing. None of us needed to be told that it hadn't been created by any natural force. There were no damn mountains of any kind in Indiana.

Especially not mountains with temples on top.

It was large enough that we could see part of it from where we stood—a soaring, many-columned thing perched precariously on the plateau at the mountain's zenith. In a twisted way, it reminded me of the Lincoln Memorial, as if someone had built a tainted caricature. The glittering silver threads of a waterfall poured off the sheer northern side and vaporized into mist that cloaked the base of the landmass.

We looked at each other. "This is our stop," I said.

"Don't kill me for this," Frank said, "but it's pretty fucking cool."

Steph shot him the dirtiest look I'd ever seen, even from her. "You're a pig," she told him. "Don't compliment the enemy."

The vampire threw his hands up. "I was speaking from a friggin' *architectural* standpoint. Sue me for thinking the scumbag's mountaintop lair is a slick piece of work."

"That's an idea," Steph said. She turned to Jules. "You're a lawyer, aren't you?"

Frank groaned. "Give me a break, woman. I swear I can't go ten minutes without you busting my balls."

Jules stifled a laugh. "I'm not that kind of lawyer," she said apologetically. "I can definitely refer you, though."

"Excellent." The FBI agent threw a pointed glance in Frank's direction. "I'll keep that in mind. For the future."

"All right." I clapped my hands to get everyone's attention. "Let me interrupt you for a minute so we can discuss the game plan." I gestured toward the temple on the peak. "We currently stand on the long approach to Delano's temple. This is where we've arranged to meet with the team from D.C. When they get here, we'll go in and assassinate that slimy fucker. Then we call in his men after word gets out that Delano is dead because the shit will hit the fan in a major way. Are we all clear?" A murmur of general assent rippled around the circle. I smiled. "Good. Now, I guess we wait."

Idle conversation resumed. I looked at my watch. We had actually turned up a little later than we'd arranged but there was no sign of the smoking man or any of his cohorts. I hoped they hadn't run into anything meaner than ogres or bigger than giants on their way.

*Fret not, Victoria. This smoking man strikes me as one who lives by his own parameters. I have no doubt he will get by just fine.*

I frowned. "Somehow, that doesn't make me feel any better." Everyone else seemed to enjoy the downtime, so I tried to force a veneer of calm over my expression. Deacon sauntered over and slipped an arm around my waist.

"Hurry up and wait," he said. "It's always the way."

I folded my arms but a corner of my cool façade had already slipped. He had a way of bringing all my feelings to the forefront, whether I liked it or not. "He should be here by now," I said. "It's not like we were early."

Deacon looked at the road and down the way we had come. "Yeah, well, he's on bureaucracy time. You know as well as I do that they do whatever they want, however they want. Everyone else's schedules can pack it off to hell."

I made a noise of disgust and irritation. Hours of uninterrupted introspection in the truck had already frayed my nerves and now, I felt like I was tightrope walking along power lines.

"We're not meeting up for a fucking lunch date," I said.

He rubbed my shoulder. "I know that, and trust me, I know how big a deal this is. But we need his help, Vic. There's no way we can go in alone and expect to come out of there alive. Nobody's said as much, but everyone knows it. We have to wait." He turned to face me directly. "Take a deep breath, babe. It's gonna be okay. They were probably held up dealing with the same kind of dumb bullshit we ran into."

I gazed into Deacon's dark eyes and felt the monumental pressure of the world fall away for a few seconds. All the storm clouds that had gradually accumulated in my head blew away. I leaned in and put my arms around him.

"That's the first time you've ever called me babe," I mumbled into his chest.

"Uh, yeah. Yeah, it is." He hesitated. "Too weird?"

I tilted my head to the side, my cheek against his amazingly solid pecs, and grinned at him. "I'll be honest. If you were any other guy, I'd have knocked your block off the moment it came out of your mouth. But I can let it slide this time."

"Thanks." He touched my cheek. "I'm pretty attached to this old block."

"Yeah." I stood on my toes and kissed him gently. "Me too."

The minutes transformed slowly into hours as we waited under the vast Indiana sky. The sun, which had hung low over the horizon on arrival, disappeared completely behind the opaque mass of Delano's mountain and a wave of fresh cold swept in. Frank, Maya, and Steph, who had waged snowball wars in the dregs of the afternoon light, had to stop for lack of visibility.

I took another peek at my watch. "Where the hell is this guy?" I asked out loud to no one in particular. "He turns up everywhere else uninvited. He should be here by now."

*While I understand your impatience, I maintain that it would be unwise to attempt the operation without the agreed-upon reinforcements present,* said Marcus.

"I'm not saying you're wrong about that but look at how much time we've lost." I jabbed my hand at the rapidly darkening sky. "Delano could be doing anything in there while we dick around in some shitty cornfield and wait for our buddies. By the time we get in there, it could be too late."

*I am confident that we would know the moment our window of opportunity closed. Delano has lost much of his subtlety in recent weeks.*

"Sure, but that doesn't mean we can stand here with our thumbs up our asses." I kicked at a clump of snow.

"Maybe he decided it would be better to go in at night," Maya suggested and hugged herself against the cold.

"Then he shouldn't have told us to meet him in the fucking afternoon." I pinched the bridge of my nose and willed my temper not to flare. "Sorry, I didn't mean to snap. I can't help feeling that we've been stood up."

"I get it." The Were adjusted her coat. "We have waited here a long time."

Brax shoved open the door of the truck where he and Jules had been holed up together. "Are we doing this or not?" he asked as he strode across the frozen ground. Jules was right behind him.

I looked toward the foreboding outline of the mountain which somehow seemed darker than the surrounding night. Delano's temple blazed with lights like an arrogant, defiant beacon. "You know what?" I cracked my knuckles and then my neck. "Screw it. We're going in."

"That's what I'm talking about!" The demon grinned, obviously ready for action. I made a brief survey of my small, dedicated team. Maya gave me a thumbs-up. Steph checked her gun. Frank shrugged and nodded.

Deacon said, "That might not be the best idea."

All eyes went instantly to him, including mine. I refused to admit that his sudden lack of faith made me both hurt and angry—he didn't have to say that in front of the whole crew, at least. "I got this, remember?" I asked pointedly.

"For the second time, it's not because of you," he replied. "Do you really want to make this guy into a wild-card out here? Let's say we leave, he shows up, and we're gone. He could make all kinds of crazy assumptions about why he thinks we didn't show. If he tells his network we double-crossed him, we'll be in serious trouble."

*Deacon's concerns have merit,* said Marcus. *This enigmatic man could quickly turn into an uncontrollable variable.*

"We'll leave him a note," I said tersely. "Piss it into the damn snow for all I care. It's a risk I'm willing to take. We need to do this, and we need to do it now."

"Hear, hear," Brax said gruffly. "Are you in or out, Feddie?"

Deacon held his hands up in surrender. "Okay. You're the boss. I'm all the way in."

"So am I," said Jules.

Brax and I glanced at her.

"Don't look at me like that," she said stubbornly. "You'll need someone to get out and get help should things go south." The fiery determination in her eyes was one I'd seen a billion times over the course of our friendship. She had her mind made up.

Still, the idea of throwing her into the deep end made my stomach churn. I turned toward Brax. He wasn't happy, but he held her hand tightly. "I'll protect her," he said. "With my life."

I nodded solemnly. "I'll hold you to that." I glanced at the rest of the group. "It's time to go."

We set off across the field and directly toward the foot of the god-made mountain.

# CHAPTER TWELVE

The temple approach was a couple of miles long by the GPS's estimate, and the plan was to sneak through as much of it as possible. We remained low and quiet for the first mile, our eyes and ears alert for the slightest hint of hostile life. The area appeared to be completely devoid of anything except us. Which was great, because no matter how carefully we moved, the crunch of our boots in the snow might as well have been gunshots to my hypersensitive ears.

At the one-mile mark, the scene changed. Frosted dead leaves and a thin, crusty snowpack gave way abruptly to scorched earth littered with cinders. Not a single blade of grass grew as far as the eye could see, right up to the start of the mountain climb. The fire that had scoured the landscape had burned fast and hot before it died. Its mark was everywhere.

Brax grunted. "It looks like Asphodel, although the cold's an improvement."

"Speak for yourself," Frank said. He'd swapped his old

hat for a grey woolen winter cap that he pulled down over his ears. "I've never known any other kind of winter, and it still makes me want to jump off the Brooklyn Bridge."

A sardonic smile crept onto the demon's face. "That's what happens when you lose all your insulation."

The vampire barked out a laugh. "Asshole."

"Cool it, you pricks," Steph hissed. "Let's try to get inside before we fuck it up."

Frank dropped back to walk beside her and made a big show of checking behind her back.

"What are you doing?" she demanded.

"Looking to see if you grew wings when I wasn't looking," he said. "Those harpies could use a new recruit after what Vic did to 'em." He smiled widely and kissed her on the cheek.

"Ugh, you are such a goon." She tried not to smile but it didn't quite work. "Seriously, shut your pie hole. The closer we can get without them noticing, the better off we'll be."

Frank saluted. "Yes, ma'am." He actually *did* shut his mouth and remained close by her side. I caught Steph's eye and gave her a nod of silent approval. She winked.

The road snaked to the foot of the crag. A weird shape protruded from the sooty ashes in the shallow ditch alongside the shoulder.

Frank mentioned it first. "What the hell is that thing?" He had already veered off to take a look and we all gravitated toward his trajectory. It proved to be larger than I'd expected, and soon, I was close enough to identify the protruding piece as a limb, now stiff with rigor mortis. The muscles had shriveled inside a strangely olive-toned skin.

The vampire reached the edge of the depression and

looked down. He whistled. A moment later, I stepped beside him. There was no mistaking the corpse sprawled on the blackened dirt. Beleza's eyes were open and so was his mouth. His features clung to the gaunt frame of his skull, and his once voluminous hair was lank and dull. He had been drained and his withered husk left to rot in the open.

*A very bad omen,* Marcus intoned. *Although I am not sure Beleza could have mustered much of a fight. He was never very warlike.*

I thought about the way Beleza had clashed with me and I had to agree. Even if he had fought back, at this point, a punch was likely the same as a tickle to Delano.

"Keep going," I whispered to my team. "But be careful."

The mountain grew larger as we approached until it was all we could see. Its surface was rough and crumbly, made of stones and boulders packed in dirt. It was like Delano had simply ordered his thralls to mound up the earth as high as they could make it. I realized that it might be more treacherous to climb it than I'd expected.

The mountain itself, however, quickly became a secondary concern. Voices floated toward us through the shadows from the right. I signaled for everyone to hit the dirt. We sprawled on our stomachs and held a collective breath. The chill seeped in through the front of my coat but I waited despite the discomfort.

The voices came from a patrol unit made up of a cadre of satyrs. We heard their peals of braying laughter long before they entered striking range. Like always, they held a variety of spray-and-pray guns to their skinny chests. Most of them no longer hid their hooves. The stench of booze drifted to my nostrils—so strong that one of them must have had an open container. I shrugged, unfazed by that. A drunk enemy was a dead one.

I raised a closed fist to my crew. We held our position until the unit crossed almost directly in front of us and we ambushed them from the darkness. All but one dropped instantly. A few shots rattled off in the eerie silence, but the skirmish was over within a minute. They hadn't stood a fraction of a chance.

I knelt on the chest of the sole survivor and my blade shriveled the coarse hair that covered his throat. He was crying and snot ran down his boorish face, his fear naked in his eyes.

"I guess a good security detail wasn't in the budget," I remarked. "Tell me the best way to get inside and I might not kill you."

He sniffed and with a surprising show of boldness, sneered through his tears. "Usually, I'd make you buy me dinner first."

I drew back my hand and whipped him across the face with the butt of the *Gladius Solis,* so fast he didn't have time to flinch. "Cut the crap, Casanova," I ordered. "Murder's still on the table."

He issued a pitiful yelp as his head rolled back to center. A deep red mark bloomed on his cheekbone. The next time he spoke, blood colored his teeth, and the words were slightly garbled. "South side," he mumbled. His terrified gaze was fixed on my sword hand. "It's the weakest. They only put one patrol out there because that's where they process all the slaves."

I smiled sweetly. "See? That's all you had to say."

I knocked him out cold.

I straightened and turned to the group. "Hear that? You guys head south. Try to keep a low profile but be ready to free any slaves you see. The supply chain that feeds this place needs to be severed as quickly as possible."

"You're not coming with us?" Maya asked. She scowled her disapproved.

I shook my head. "I'll take the north side express to the temple. Delano's about to get a nasty little surprise."

"Are you crazy?" Frank erupted. "That's a one-way ticket. We're supposed to be in the shit together, Vic." The others echoed this sentiment and the volume swelled.

"There's no way we can let you go off alone," Maya insisted. "Not this time. Delano's a different breed."

"I know," I said. Strangely, all my prior anxieties had been replaced by a sense of energized serenity. It was the way I always felt when I knew I was about to get shit done. "But you'll have to trust me on this. I'll be fine, and you will be too. We'll meet up on the flip side, okay? This is a fight I need to take on my own."

"Bullshit," Brax said. "I won't fight you on this but I want you to know you're full of it." He stared hard at me and his gaze somehow seemed to pierce through the sunglasses he still wore on his face. I wondered if he knew I had thought about what both Marcus and the smoking man had said about trusting my friends too deeply. When this was all over, maybe I'd have to ask him to forgive me.

But it wasn't over yet, and we were running out of time.

"Vic, why?" Jules gave me a searching, confused look. I wanted to answer her, but the arrival of a second patrol prevented it. My team assumed battle stations in record time and channeled their emotions into a furious, whirl-wind attack. Blood and scraggly patches of satyr fur were soon scattered over the vicinity.

"You're really doing this," Steph said. She examined me closely, her face as impassive as ever.

"Yeah," I said.

She sighed. "You're one crazy bitch, but I'm rooting for you."

I smirked. "Thanks. Like I said, trust me. This is the way it has to be."

Maya came forward and hugged me with all her considerable strength. "I hate this," she said. "And I want you to know that. But I have faith that you know what you're doing."

Jules came next. She didn't say anything and her gaze, brighter than usual, remained on my face. Frank cleared his throat. "Good luck, kid," he said quietly. "I better be seeing you."

Steph laid her hand on my shoulder. "Fucking kill that son of a bitch," she said. "For all of us."

Deacon waited until the others had spoken before he pulled me aside. "Promise me you'll take care of yourself," he said. "Don't do anything stupider than usual. I need you to come through this."

I smiled. "Otherwise, you'll have to try online dating. You know, when the Internet's fixed."

He chuckled in spite of himself. "I'm gonna miss you."

"Hey." I feigned injury. "Give me a little more credit than that. I'm not dead yet."

The sadness in his eyes didn't shift, and that made me sorrier than anything else had done in a long time. I wished I could soothe his worries and tell him he was overreacting. But the truth was, I couldn't. The odds, as Marcus had said, were slim.

If I didn't win, I would die.

Deacon leaned down to place his lips against mine. I stopped him gently. "Save it for when that bastard's dead."

"I'll take that as a promise," he replied. He released me, turned back to the others, and walked away to rejoin them.

*That may have been callous of you, Victoria,* Marcus said reproachfully.

"No," I answered. "It's a little extra motivation. For both of us."

# CHAPTER THIRTEEN

The north side of the mountain was easy to locate on account of the dense mist that cloaked the face. Visibility in the cloud was sharply reduced, but I could hear the waterfall over my head and I used that to guide me. There were plenty of handholds in the face of the cliff. I didn't let the fact that they were slick with condensation deter me from my goal. As soon as I found a starting point, I pulled myself up, and the ground began to fall away as I moved steadily upward.

Gradually, the fog dissipated as well. The smell of wet earth filled my nose and frigid drops of water dripped constantly into my eyes. I trained all my focus on the climb for the first fifty feet or so until my hand gripped the top of a broad ledge. Half a second later, shards of pain knifed down my arm as someone out of my line of sight stepped hard on my fingers.

I clenched my teeth and powered through the pain to lever myself onto the ledge. A boot-clad foot lurched toward me but I caught it in one hand and rolled to the very edge of the precipice. My free arm swung into open air and I fought the powerful instinct to look down.

"Well, well." The voice that hovered above me was low and grating, the verbal equivalent of rock on rock. It belonged to a stocky, broad-faced man with stubby horns on his head. "Look what the cat dragged in."

He squared his stance and his bumpy skin reminded me of a toad.

"I dragged myself up here, thank you very much," I said. "And thanks for stepping on my fingers. You're lucky I have five others." I examined my injured hand quickly. My thumb, index, and middle fingers were swollen although they didn't hurt that much. I flexed them gingerly.

"Who are you, anyway?" I asked. My hope was that some inane small talk might allow me an opportunity to take him by surprise. The last thing I wanted was for him to raise the alarm while I was still this low on the mountain.

"Don't matter who I am," he replied as he brandished a long, thin staff. "This is as far as you'll go."

I drew the *Gladius Solis* in response. "Spoken like a true dickhead who's never met me before."

The blade illuminated his lumpy face but he didn't bat an eyelash. His staff swung at me with a speed that would have been dizzying for anyone else. I blocked his strikes with equal agility and new notches smoked on the sides of his staff.

"Nice try," I said.

The guard gritted his teeth and hunched into a brawler's posture. He attacked once more, but his weakened weapon snapped into pieces instead of making the impact he'd intended. I rammed the tip of my sword into the ground and used it to vault over him. He skidded toward the cliff edge. One foot went over and he seemed to hover a moment before the rest of his body pitched after, a prisoner to momentum. He twisted at the last minute and grabbed the ledge.

"Well, well," I said and stood over him. "Look what the cat's about to toss out." Rather than step on his fingers, I chose to cut them off. His shriek of pain transformed instantly into one of terror as he plunged to his death.

The ledge on which I found myself ran the entire way around the mountain. As far as I could tell, it served as a catwalk for the security that still seemed oddly lax. The mountain was wide enough that I knew there had to be other guards who patrolled at this level, but I didn't want to waste more time by dealing with them. I extinguished the sword and headed for the vertical path hewn out of the rock. When I craned my head back, I could pick out an obvious route, probably the most popular among Delano's personnel—and most likely also the most efficient.

Without the choking cloak of mist, the climb was actually fairly pleasant. The presence of the patrol ledges mitigated the threat of height to some extent, and I settled into a good rhythm. It hadn't taken long for my body to adjust to vertical movement. This part was easy.

"Do you have any idea what that guy was?" I asked Marcus as I pulled my way upward. "I don't remember a toad god."

*By my estimate, he was a hybrid. Perhaps a demon such as Abraxzael mixed with some other infernal creature. I expect we will see many more of these unorthodox creations as we proceed.*

*There have been misfits throughout the annals of the gods' history, often easily manipulated for a cause.*

"But now Delano's making it trendy," I muttered. "Figures."

*Delano's method manages to transfer the god's power without diluting it. I assume this is because he bypasses blood and genetics entirely.*

"Heh." I wiped my hair out of my eyes. "When in doubt, consume."

*That seems to be his rationale, yes.*

I paused briefly to get my bearings and tried to gauge how far I had yet to go. It was difficult to tell. "Even his stupid lair has to be a pain in the ass," I said.

*I am proud of you for choosing to face it alone,* said Marcus. *I am sure it was a painful conclusion to reach, but it is the wisest course of action.*

"I hope so." There was a knot in my stomach that simply wouldn't go away. "I know you're positive, and I'm glad about that, at least. But no matter which way I look at it, I feel like I might've made a horrible mistake. It's like the classic, 'what if he wants to split us up' kind of worry. Like, maybe I played right into his hands."

*As you said before, this is a risk that must be taken. I cannot overemphasize Delano's greatness, as much as I despise doing so. His current form is superior to anything I have ever witnessed, either on this earth or in the realm of the gods. The spirits of your friends, strong as they may be, would be crushed by his mere presence.*

I frowned. "Dude, what the fuck? You don't have to write me a poem about the guy. He's the one we hate."

*I believe he has met his match in you. You, too, are like*

nothing I have beheld in my ages of life among humanity. If Delano is the darkness, you are the light. And you will snuff him out.

"That's more like it," I said.

He went on. *Even if you should fail, the bards will sing your praises for eternity—a hero the likes of which the world has never known and will never know again.*

I laughed and shook my head slightly. "And we're back to no good. I need you to be my hype man right now, Marcus. Talk about my honor and all that other shit you love to go on about. I don't know about you, but I'd rather stay off the bards' medieval pop charts."

*I thought you would enjoy being the subject of a drinking song.*

"Not as much as I'd enjoy living to a ripe old age. What kind of woman do you take me for, anyway?"

*The kind who is capable of bringing down the god to end all gods.*

I fumbled upward and grasped the next ledge. "Good answer."

Steeling my nerves for whatever I might see, I hauled myself up and over.

At first, I encountered nothing but a weird, musty smell. I stood still, my sword at the ready, and peered into the inky well of shadows in front of me. The wall went back much farther, almost like a cave. The sounds of shuffling and creepy, non-verbal moans met my ears. Shapes like bodies materialized from the void. I felt the hair stand up on my arms and the back of my neck.

"Oh, hell no," I whispered.

Shambling toward me was a small herd of Beleza's

former henchmen, but they were shells of their former selves. Gone were the rich tans and toned muscles, now replaced by greyish, sagging skin stretched over skeletons. Like their late god, they had shriveled significantly. The tatters of their skimpy underwear clung to their hips. They moved en masse, their eyes milky and blank and their jaws slack. And in the middle, guiding them along, was their shepherd. I recognized the tall, gruesomely thin figure from a parking lot in a small town outside the Delaware Water Gap. The last I'd seen of him, he was running away as a horde of zombies came between us.

"You," said the god. His mouth twitched into the semblance of a smile. "How serendipitous it is to see you again." The words blew over me in a rotten wind. "Tell me. Are you still in the business of killing gods?"

"Yes." I withdrew the *Gladius Solis* as proof. "And business is booming."

He chuckled. A weird note of some emotion floated underneath. Sadness maybe, or wistfulness. "Once, I would have mocked you for daring to think you could kill me." He fixed his vacant eyes on my face, and white sparks seemed to dance in colorless pools. "Now, I can only hope you will succeed."

He raised his hands and thrust them forward. The members of his horde rushed at me.

*This is most unusual,* Marcus remarked in a tone of voice that made me think he really meant to say, "fucked up." I swept my sword in a quick, brutal circle and cleaved the first wave of Beleza's fallen followers in half. They clattered to the ground and froze weakly into pitiful approximations of statues. But those final forms were brittle and unsustainable, even in death. They crumbled beneath the feet of their brethren, who were cut down just as quickly.

I looked through the melee at the zombie god. He stood listlessly at the back and went through the motions of directing the remaining mob. I slashed at the final few and advanced on the corporeal specter. He was at least eight feet tall, his head stooped beneath the ceiling of the hollowed cavern.

"You can do better than that," I said. "Come on." My brain told me I was wasting time I didn't have, but the god's utter sense of defeat fascinated me. I'd never seen one beaten down and yet still alive.

"There is no use in trying," he told me. "For the final time, I have been passed over and relegated into a position of insignificance. If I endure, I shall be forced to bear witness to Delano's gross abuse of the power he never earned. I would rather be obliterated than exist this way, a roach in a hall of kings."

"Damn," I said. "You're still an asshole, though."

He shrugged and seemed to acknowledge the statement. "For my actions, I do not and cannot repent. Humanity is a plague to be purged. But you?" The god extended a long finger as if to touch me. "You are more than that, for a simple human cannot kill even a god such as I. Still, I have yearned to meet you again."

I lifted the sword. "Fight me, and I'll kill you."

"Why should I fight?" asked the god. "It would only prolong the end which I desire." He stared emptily into my face. "No. There is no more struggle to be had. There is only ruin." The folds of the tattered cloak swept open to reveal the black heart I hadn't pierced in our first fight. He was silent, motionless, and docile. I summoned the blade and stepped toward the broken god. When I was close enough, he knelt and closed his eyes.

"I don't know where you're going," I said. "But I hope it sucks."

The sword entered the heart in one swift movement. Its beat stuttered.

"Thank you," he breathed. The heart convulsed and evaporated into nothing. The rest of the body rapidly followed suit. In a matter of seconds, all that was left was the ragged cloak.

"I think I like it better when they fight me," I said.

CHAPTER FOURTEEN

Near the top of the mountain, the flow of cascading water became more of a torrent. I had to scramble to the side in order to circumvent most of the flood, but my arms and the front of my jacket were still soaked when I crested the final lip of the topmost plateau. I stood there for a moment to catch my breath and shake rivulets off my fingers as I gazed at the soaring spires of the temple.

Someone was clearly compensating for something.

I walked forward and scanned the vicinity for patrols. The entire plateau was deserted, except for one corner that protruded over the cliff face. A large boulder sat there, secured by chains that had been wound around the body of a fish-tailed, androgynous being. It was still alive and writhed in agony, its mouth twisted open in an everlasting scream.

The creature's glimmering, scaled torso had been pierced by a spear, and the start of a thunderous waterfall poured from the wound. I looked down over the hundreds of feet I had climbed and realized that the water I'd seen on the way up was only runoff. The main fall dropped into the surging thread of a river far below.

*This is horrific,* Marcus proclaimed, and his words dripped with disgust.

I took an extra moment to examine the wretched water god with some amount of pity, but even if I'd wanted to, there was nothing I could do—not without announcing my presence. I turned away and walked toward the grand entrance to the temple's main hall. The doors were already open and loomed above me. I felt judged as I passed between them.

Only dead silence lay on the other side. The hall was incredibly long, its vaulted ceilings painted with scores of swirling, colorful murals. The scenes burned with violent energy and depicted portrait after portrait of blood, death, and war.

I was hyperaware of the sounds created by my own body. My pulse thrummed in my ears. Each breath seemed to rush in and out of my lungs like a gale-force wind. Echoes danced from every corner of the vast chamber.

Delano's hall was furnished with nothing besides an altar at the far end and pillars that rose to the roof, apparently with the sole purpose of enshrining another enormous door. Halfway across the creepily empty space, I noticed that each of the pillars was made of another conquered god.

I cursed under my breath. A few of them were unlike anything I'd ever seen before—or anything I could comprehend. They were ancient, ornate behemoths, frozen in the moments of their demise. One was missing its left eye.

"He killed all of these," I said softly, unable to suppress the automatic rush of awe.

*He has made them a part of his soul,* Marcus said. *They are dead and yet they live in him.*

The thought of so many stolen souls locked up in Delano's body made my stomach do a barrel roll. The corpse-pillars lined both sides of the center, all the way to that door. As I stared at it and wondered where it might lead, it opened. I half expected a decoy or an extended lead-up, but there was absolutely no mistaking the man—the myth, the legend.

I grimaced. "Someone's been busy."

Delano stepped down from the elevated threshold he had just crossed and onto the altar's gleaming platform. The portal boomed shut behind him and its impact reverberated through the stillness. The changes in his form were apparent despite the distance. He had attained Beleza's bronzed skin and some of his tone and height and a bright, baleful jewel glittered in the hollow between his eyes. A slender, whip-like tail curled around the backs of his legs and ended in a brutal barb. The pale eyes he'd always had now revealed slit pupils. His wings folded along the curve of his spine.

Neither of us said a word but our gazes locked. The air grew frosty, along with my mood. I already itched to be done with him.

"Game over, Delano," I said and raised my voice to be heard at the other end of the hall. "You bought as much time as you could, and I'll admit, it was a lot. But it's running out now. You're down to minutes. Soon, it'll be seconds. And then, you'll be finished for good. I've come to tie up Kronin's last loose end."

Delano smiled. "Brave words," he said. "From a stupid woman." He ambled slowly toward me and talked all the while. "I waited so long for you to understand, Vic, and still, you won't oblige me. Allow me to enlighten you now that we're here, face to face at last. Humans are weak. They are frail, breakable, and full of little more than blood and water. I have seen human bones ground into dust, their skin flayed off and left to dry as hide in the wind."

"So humans are weak, which means we deserve to die?" I asked.

He laughed. "It means you're irrelevant to my plans. I am stronger than any god who has traversed any earth. I am the sum of all that is mighty. The end of the world for many. And the sole reward for standing in defiance of such power is suffering the likes of which you cannot hope to imagine."

His smile expanded into a grin. "But there is another way," he said. "For I am a merciful lord and master. Follow me as you followed the coward Kronin into the futile darkness that now encompasses your planet. Fall to your knees and surrender. Offer supplication like all the others before you, and you will see that Kronin was but a speck of dust. I have become everything."

I scowled. "Here's something I learned a long time ago, dick-face. All gods can die. And you still don't have this." The *Gladius Solis* slipped into my hand and blazed to life. "It's a power you'll never be able to master."

The god laughed as if he found me genuinely funny. "I beg to differ," he said. "The sword of the gods is only as strong as its wielder. Why do you think it allowed Kronin to die? And now, the one who wields its blade is only human. A fitting end to Kronin's sordid legacy. He loved your kind so much and finally, your kind will fail him. *You will fail him.*"

He stopped several paces away. "Come," he said. "Let's prove once and for all that you were never worthy to wield the Hero-King's blade."

He spread his arms, and the great black wings on his back unfurled in tandem.

*Victoria, it is now or never.*

I launched into the attack and a full-fledged war cry broke from my lungs. The sword traced a fiery trail in my wake. Flames danced along its edges and its power already flooded my hands and arms with glowing light.

The gap separating Delano and I disappeared in a flash —and then he was gone too. Black vapor clouded my vision to dissipate and condense ten yards to the left.

"You missed," he said. "Now, it's my turn."

His wings whipped up a storm at ground level. I was shoved backward, my feet unable to find purchase on the smooth stone floor. A pillar caught my body in the stiff embrace of a dead god. High above, Delano opened his mouth wide. White-hot flames surged from his throat and rocketed toward me at breakneck speed.

"Are you kidding me with this shit?" I shouted. "When did he swallow a fucking dragon?"

*Keep your wits about you,* Marcus warned. *Any strike has the potential to kill.*

His warning galvanized me into action, and I dropped instantly and rolled to the side. With a faint sizzle, the water still in my jacket evaporated immediately and part of the hem burned away. The exposed skin of my cheeks and chin felt seared and raw simply from the intensity of the heat.

I crouched behind the next pillar and poked my head out of cover as Delano disappeared yet again. Before I had the chance to try to pinpoint where he'd gone, his hand was on the back of my neck and long nails dug into my flesh.

Instinctively, I twisted and lashed out with the *Gladius Solis.* My skin tore like tissue paper, but I barely registered the pain. The sword bit deep into Delano's side, but the wound it inflicted might as well have been a scratch. He hauled me off my feet by the back of my clothes, and in the next moment, I hurtled forward, literally in the air. When I finally landed, stars exploded in the void behind my clenched eyelids.

He had flung me around like a damn toy.

"This is how your quest ends," Delano said. His shadow loomed over me as I struggled to stand. He reached out and caressed my face before he gripped it in iron fingers. "With humiliation, torment, and the abject ruins of your dignity."

"I'm not dead yet." I spat in his eye and leapt up to drive the point of my sword through his chest. Again, the edge somehow did no more than graze him.

He seized me by the sword arm and his skin hardened into shining, unbreakable rock. "You will be," he said. My body catapulted over his shoulder with all the resistance of a ragdoll, but I managed to right myself and hit the ground running. We'd switched places during the course of the fight, and I saw the door on the altar directly ahead.

I bolted toward it.

"This isn't working!" I told Marcus. "I need to find a better position to try to reset things more in my favor. It's the only chance I've got."

*Would that I had my earthly body and could stand beside you against our common foe,* he lamented. *Feel no fear, Victoria. Whatever happens here, I shall see you at the end.*

I vaulted up onto the grand altar and thrust headlong through the door. Delano's mocking laughter followed me up the staircase I found behind it.

"Kronin's sword reveals another coward," he sang, his tone twisted by sadistic glee.

I didn't stop. I couldn't. The steps seemed to ascend forever but I finally burst through the top into the cold night air that slashed instantly through my damaged coat. I was headed straight for a low wall that marked the edge of the roof and I backpedaled in an effort to give myself as much room as possible. The formerly empty temple plateau spread out before me, now crowded with Delano's worshippers. Soundlessly, they watched. The head start I'd attempted to gain was lost in the fraction of a second during which I attempted to avoid hurtling over the edge of the roof.

He came up behind me and clamped a hand on my right bicep. "Look upon those fortunate enough to know when they are bested."

As I tried to pull away, he spun me and slapped the back of his hand across my face. I careened helplessly into the wall. The breath expelled sharply from my chest and my teeth literally rattled in my skull.

Delano stormed at me, his pale eyes full of unadulterated rage. The hatred radiated off him like a toxic cloud. This was the end he'd planned for me, but he hadn't killed me yet.

And I'd spotted a weakness.

The sliver had been almost invisible before, situated across the left side of his chest over his heart. It was the only flaw in his obsessively perfect form, and I had a fleeting moment to take my shot. As the mega-god approached, I let the *Gladius Solis* fly like an arrow, straight and true.

*Bullseye.*

At least, it should have been. After I released the hilt, a shell began to thicken over that single weakness. New skin obscured the sliver and grew hard and reflective. It was still thin when the blade impacted but not weak enough. The sword protruded from where it hit, stopped in its deadly assault.

Delano screamed in pain, but it was no death rattle. He didn't disintegrate into a pile of ash but instead, grabbed the sword in both hands. He yanked it out and at first, I believed that the blade had receded, perhaps in defiance. Then I realized it had simply turned black. He thrust it aloft as his maniacal, bellowed laughter shattered the starry sky.

When he had finished gloating, he turned toward me. "The sword of the gods," he said. "The *Gladius Solis* is as strong as its wielder. Consider this a demonstration."

He rushed at my position against the wall. The sword's black blade cut a cruelly familiar arc.

"You have gifted me the key to victory," he said. His face contorted into a wild, sickening rictus. "For that, I thank you."

I pushed myself to my feet. No way would I die sitting down and backed into a dead end. If I really had to die, I'd do it like I'd done everything else for the past half a decade —by my own fucking rules.

*Remember how I taught you,* Marcus said. He spoke gently, not urgently. *Fists up. Protect your face.*

I stepped up to Delano's challenge and took a swing. He blocked it with his left hand and lunged and sliced with his right. I ducked back, which spared my torso but my leg was not so lucky. The *Gladius Solis* cut into me as if I was no more than a ghost, exactly the way it had done hundreds of times by my hand. I hit the ground before I knew for sure I'd been wounded.

It had been a long time since I last felt pain I couldn't bear. The corrupted sword retaught me the meaning of agony. I would have severed my own limb to make it stop.

"Yes," Delano declared. He latched onto me. "It is done."

He hauled me over the top of the wall and shoved me into open air. Discordant jeers rose to meet me. I stared into the sea of faces and saw those of my own people, captured and herded to the front. They all wore masks of horror.

Delano hissed into my ear. "I told you the consequences of defiance. The time for enforcement has come."

He leapt down to the temple plateau. All I heard was the rush of water and the fiery beat of the wound in my leg.

Marcus said softly, *I am sorry, Victoria.*

I was too.

"Do you see this?" Delano's voice boomed at the crowd. "I have brought the final sacrifice—indeed, the ultimate sacrifice. Who better than I to receive the blood of the god-killer as tribute? Behold as the slayer of gods is slain."

He threw me down beside the boulder and raised the *Gladius Solis.*

"Hell no!" The shout rang out like a gunshot and roused me to attention. A rush of adrenaline beat back my pain as Delano was knocked aside. I shoved to my feet as my head spun and I stumbled unevenly toward the crowd and away from the seething god. One of the guards stopped my progress

*Clear your mind, Victoria. Stay sharp. You have not been bested yet.*

I sucked in a deep breath and delivered a punch. This one landed, at least, and my captor fell onto his back. I lunged to kick, claw, and pummel him with every ounce of strength left in my body. The whole world faded into nothing. All that existed was me in a fight for my life.

Oh, and Marcus was there too.

He shouted in my head to fill my brain with raw energy and guided my aim. *Take out his eyes. Use the environment to your advantage. You can defeat him if you are clever about it.*

I tried my best to follow his coaching, but it was impossible to ignore the fact that I didn't possess the sword. The guard who fought me was fast, strong, and far too durable for me to defeat in my current condition. Once he'd wrestled the upper hand away from me, he'd backed me up to the cliff.

Five heavy knuckles straight to the jaw sent me in a not so graceful arc out and over the waterfall. As I started to plummet, I caught a glimpse of the figure who'd saved me from Delano's clutches sprawled on the rock beneath the point of the *Gladius Solis.*

My heart leapt into my throat. There was no mistaking that silhouette, even in defeat.

*Deacon.*

Darkness enveloped my whole body. I no longer felt the cold or the pain. I knew I continued to drop toward the river, but it was a blank awareness. All I thought and all I saw was my love, ripped away before my eyes. The moments I spent in suspension above the water were each small eternities in themselves. I could have imagined Deacon forever.

But the water came up to embrace me and everything washed away.

# CHAPTER FIFTEEN

A ragged cough brought me back to consciousness. I lay on the bank of the swiftly running river on my stomach and continued to hack up a delightful mixture of bile and dirty water. The back of my throat burned like hell, but the sensation paled in comparison to the angry rebuke from the wound in my leg. Rolling over to look at it was torture, and the sight didn't exactly fill me with hope.

Black veins spidered outward from the deep gash, which throbbed in time with my pulse. I groaned and leaned forward to expel more gross water from my stomach.

"You're lucky to be alive," someone said.

I jerked my head up and as my vision greyed out, I almost puked again. The smoking man stood and gazed down at me. A cigarette burned between his fingers.

Immediately, I saw red. "You fucking prick! Where the hell were you?" The words were as venomous as I could make them but still weak.

He took a slow, insolent drag. "You were supposed to wait for me."

If I'd had the strength, I might have murdered his ass on the spot. "We waited for fucking hours!" I yelled hoarsely. "Until we couldn't take it anymore. This whole shitty, stupid mess is your fault, asshole. I hope it rots you from the inside out." The tirade exhausted me, but I refused to let up. "We lost everyone. Do you not understand that, or do you simply not care? I'm the only one who got out. I'm all that's left. I hope it's what you fucking wanted, you dogshit bastard."

He merely stared at me, continued to smoke nonchalantly, and allowed me to shout until I wheezed.

At last, after I'd put my head down to catch my breath, he said, "It *is* my fault. But not for the reasons you think."

"What...the hell...does that mean?" I stared at him from my prone position on the wet bank while I fought for both strength and control. I felt like I'd been beaten with a thousand baseball bats. My leg was a constant harsh drumbeat in the background.

"I was wrong," he said simply. "I believed you were strong enough to defeat Delano. Needless to say, you are not—not now. I admit I underestimated him. He has assimilated more power than I ever imagined possible. For my miscalculations, we have paid a high price."

"I paid," I growled. "You didn't lose shit. Not a man down, not a hair out of your gnarly-ass beard. I paid for it all." That last image of Deacon flashed across my consciousness, and I forced it deep down into a mental lockbox.

"Yes." The smoking man nodded. "And now I know the truth. I have seen what we truly face."

I propped myself up on my elbows and spat out dirt and gravel. My mouth tasted like I'd licked the inside of an old well. "I can beat him," I croaked. "I can." But the conviction was no longer there. I didn't need to be told that I hadn't come close.

He responded with another nod. His eyes were trained on me, illuminated by the moonlight. They were an icy, pearly blue.

*I have said it so many times,* Marcus piped up suddenly. *Still, it bears repeating. There is nothing—not a single thing in any realm, god or human—that compares to the beast that Delano has become.*

"Oh," I mumbled. "You're still here." The sentences sounded waterlogged and miserable, but I felt great relief.

*Victoria, if water was all it took to separate us, you would never have made it this far.*

I laughed weakly. The effort hurt my chest. "Jerk."

"There is a way," the smoking man said. He lit a new cigarette although I hadn't seen him toss the last butt. "It is a last-ditch effort. A Hail Mary, if you will."

"Now you break out the cryptic comments," I said with a frown. "What kind of swamp-alien code-speak bullshit is this?"

He gave me a look equal parts stern and amused. "There is no code, only a destination—one where no human has set foot for millennia." He slipped a tablet out from under his coat, set it down on the grimy bank, and nudged it toward me. I craned my neck to look at the screen.

A map?

I frowned again and shot the smoking jackass a puzzled glance. He puffed out a white cloud in response. Grumbling a little, I pulled a hand free and pinched the screen to zoom out. My fingers left dirty wet streaks on the glass. A word showed up beside my thumb.

Nepal.

I zoomed out some more. The Himalayas. The marked location seemed practically dead center amid the famous mountain range.

"What the fuck?" I asked.

I received no answer, and when I looked up to ask again, the smoking man had gone.

"Damn it to hell," I said and pounded my fist in the river muck. "I am *over* this shit."

After a few moments, I gathered my strength and stood. I put the tablet under my arm, not caring that my sopping clothes dripped all over the screen. He'd at least been considerate enough to slap a waterproof case on the thing.

My head hurt. My face hurt where Delano had slapped me. My leg *really* hurt, and the ache was deep down in there like the bone was made of pain. There was definitely a part of me that had been beaten to the core back there at the temple. But a bigger part—the part that kept me walking—knew I had no choice. I'd failed too hard and left too much behind. Yeah, I was fucked up six ways to Sunday. I'd gotten the shit kicked out of me publicly.

But I was determined to get back to the temple, no matter what. Delano had something that belonged to me.

# CHAPTER SIXTEEN

The wet cold seeped down to my bones as I stumbled half-blind through the burned-out field and away from the monstrous, towering outline of Delano's mountain. My soaked clothes plastered against my body and left an erratic trail of water droplets behind me. Ice crystals had already begun to form along the strands of my hair. I couldn't feel my toes, my fingers, or the tip of my nose.

It felt as wrong as hell to be headed in this direction. Every fiber of my being screamed at me to turn around and haul ass back to the temple. The memory of Deacon splayed out on the plateau, the *Gladius Solis* poised to strike his heart, was seared into my mind's eye. I wanted to save him. I needed to save him.

It hurt beyond description to know I left him behind. But I also knew it was the only way. I had undeniably had the shit kicked out of me—and the painful truth was that Delano hadn't even had to try. No way could I simply run back there and expect things to go differently the second time around. Somehow, I needed to gain the upper hand.

Deacon could be dead for all I knew. Delano's intentions weren't hard to guess. I directed all my attention ahead and tried to shove those thoughts from my mind. Soon, I'd return for him and he would be right where I left him. It was the only reality I could bring myself to accept.

The festering rage kept me warm on my way through the barren winter night despite the cold air that knifed through my lungs. My face withered into a semi-permanent scowl. I glanced at the tablet still clutched in my numb hands. Fuck the smoking man and his damn cigarettes. Fuck Nepal, fuck the Himalayas, and fuck the incessant throb of the wound in my leg.

The elaborate strategies of the past that we'd pored over for hours had all gotten me jack shit. It was time to revert to sheer simplicity. Brute force. All I needed was backup—once I had it, we'd come back in, guns blazing, and we wouldn't leave until Delano was dead.

I could barely see my own hand in front of my face as I dragged my injured leg through the pitch-black field. Still, I had a decent sense of where we had started and where I needed to go to get back there. I staggered wearily through the darkness, closed my eyes, and shoved all my concentration into simply moving forward. No thoughts and no feelings were allowed. There would be time for that later.

The two-mile approach felt like ten during my retreat. I relaxed a little when I felt the snowpack beneath my feet. One more mile to go. I wouldn't be home free, but I'd be a hell of a lot closer.

When I heard the distinct crunch of footprints in crusty snow, I grimaced. "I'm already fucking running away. What more do these assholes want?"

But whoever it was, they were in my way. I dropped into a crouch and crept a little closer as I strained to see what lay ahead. Two humanoid shapes moved purposefully across the snow, obviously patrolling the perimeter. I didn't recall encountering anyone out there on the way in. Maybe Delano still tried to stomp me out while he knew he still had the chance. Like the coward he was, I thought acidly.

But instead of the *Gladius Solis* on my hip, what I had was a busted leg and clothes that had now almost frozen to my body. Even I wasn't crazy enough to try this fight. I turned with every intention to avoid this particular encounter. My shitty balance on that wounded leg, however, had other plans. Before I really had a chance to comprehend what had happened, I was on my face atop a rough pillow of ice crystals. The patrolmen were on me by the time I managed to roll over.

They were standard-issue vamps and their greyish skin held a washed-out look against the winter landscape. Each grabbed hold of an arm and shoved me deeper into the snow.

"Look at that," one of them said and grinned until his fangs caught the watery moonlight. "It's been a long time since we found a little snack wandering around these parts."

The other one chuckled. He leered into my face. "It's about damn time. I'm *starving*." He lifted a skinny hand and brushed the crystallizing strands of hair out of my face. "I bet a pretty thing like you has some sweet blood running through those veins."

I spat at him. Although valiant, it was a weak effort and he simply laughed again. His buddy suddenly grabbed him by the shoulder. "Hey, wait! I know you." His eyes burned with pure, vicious greed. "You're the one Delano is looking for!"

"Well, maybe he should've killed me on the first try," I answered.

They yanked me to my feet. As soon as I had some range of motion back, I twisted away from their grip and lashed out with my fists. The vamps were quick, but even in my current condition, I managed to be faster. The knuckles on my right hand connected solidly with a jawbone. The guy's head snapped back.

He growled. "When I'm done with you, bitch, you're gonna wish we were allowed to kill you." His narrow, bony shoulder jammed into my stomach and briefly knocked the wind out of me. I kicked as hard as I could. The toe of my boot struck bone, and I immediately kicked out again.

The first vamp cursed. "You damn devil woman! Be a good girl now and come with us." He struck me across the face so hard I saw stars and the color leaked out of my vision for a second. I felt all my limbs go slack. He hitched me forward and prepared to throw me over his shoulder. As he lifted me by the waist, I rammed my knee up into his chest and he buckled. I might've followed suit, but his buddy caught me by the back of the jacket.

"It looks like someone ought to teach you a lesson," he sneered. His fist landed under my left eye, but instead of recoiling like he expected, I seized his wrist and broke it. He released a howl of pain. I held on to his arm even as he tore at me with the claws on his good hand and raked trails of blood down my cheek. Finally, I planted my foot into his ribs and he careened backward to drop into the snow. The broken wrist flapped uselessly at his side.

I now stood over him, my boot poised to crush his chest. For a couple of seconds, his bloodshot eyes registered the uncertainty and the fear to which I'd become accustomed. But his expression flipped instantly. Without warning, he grabbed my leg with all the strength he could muster and anchored me in place.

"What the—" Caught by surprise, I wavered. The joint of my knee twisted and a searing pain blazed through the cap. "You son of a bitch!"

I lunged forward to throw my weight down on his heart, but the other goon leapt onto my back from behind. We both toppled forward. A crack was quickly followed by a weird, raspy groan and I found myself face to face with a brand-new corpse.

The vampire under my boot had gotten his chest reshaped after all.

I rolled onto the ground and thrashed furiously to escape the second vamp. He was a tenacious bastard and had driven his claws into the backs of my shoulders like meat hooks. Fortunately, at this point, I was practically frozen solid from my trip down the river and I couldn't feel much of anything—even the momentary agony in my knee had numbed—until a clammy hand wound around my throat and tightened its grip.

A new wave of panicked adrenaline surged through me. I threw myself back against the rock-solid dirt in an attempt to bash his head in or snap his neck, whichever happened first. After a few unsuccessful attempts, I grew impatient and simply smashed the back of my head into his nose as hard as I could.

The hand on my neck finally loosened and he sprawled backward onto the snow. I sat up, gasped, then turned and pinned him down.

"You'll never get away," he slurred through the torrent of blood from his broken nose. "Delano has his whole army looking for you. They'll smoke you out like—"

I snapped his neck mid-sentence, struggled to my feet, and stumbled away into the darkness. The brief rush of energy I'd felt in the fight ebbed fast. Drops of blood scattered behind me. My eyelids felt heavy and I knew I was at the end of my rope.

*Press on, Victoria. You do not have far to go.* Marcus spoke his encouragement calmly but there was an urgent undertone. He knew as well as I did that there was no way I'd be able to take Delano on in this condition. I'd had my shot and I failed. I blew it. The only place left for me to go was back to the truck. All the reinforcements in the world couldn't help me now.

The one thing Delano wasn't able to take away from me was the nectar in my veins. By the time I finally saw the trucks still parked where we'd left them, the worst of the bleeding had more or less abated. The cold still dragged my every movement and the cut from the *Gladius Solis* continued to throb, but the rest of me at least hurt a little less. I climbed numbly into the driver's seat and fumbled for the key. I didn't expect to find it, but there it was, tucked deep in my pocket. I frowned at it for a moment and wondered how the hell it had stayed put, especially during my little raft trip downstream.

After a few bemused moments, I decided not to look a gift horse in the mouth and shoved the key into the ignition. The engine grumbled for a moment or two but it turned over reluctantly.

*What is your next course of action?* Marcus asked. He sounded like he didn't think there was much left to do but tactfully left those thoughts unspoken.

"What else?" I pulled the smoking man's tablet out of my coat. The screen blinked on, still set to the map he'd shown me. "I'm going to the fucking Himalayas."

## CHAPTER SEVENTEEN

The drone of the tiny airplane's propeller filled my head as I sat in the back and made every effort not to look out the window. Strong winds buffeted the craft from every side. The sky was nothing more than an ocean of grey mist and huge, heavy raindrops spattered against the glass. Once or twice, I swore I caught a glimpse of a far-off flash of lightning.

The seat restraints were tight across my lap and chest, but I still pitched and rolled with every gust. My stomach constantly threatened to auto-eject out my nose. I hadn't eaten at all that morning, and for once, I was glad. I was also relieved that there were no other passengers besides me—not that there was much room. The only empty seat was right beside me, squeezed in alongside the opposite window. It was hard to imagine that the plane could carry the weight of another person.

The aircraft dipped to the side and almost knocked me horizontal. I clutched the seat straps for dear life and shut my eyes tightly. Up front, the pilot and co-pilot chatted back and forth in a language I didn't even recognize. The glow of the cockpit dials provided the only light, and that wasn't much. I tried to pretend that they sounded confident, like everything would be fine and they'd done this crap a million times, but there was no way to disguise their agitation. Brief periods of silence were shattered by bursts of nervous talk, and switches flipped intermittently.

None of it reassured me at all.

We nose-dived a little. My stomach jerked and went into freefall for two seconds. In the privacy of my own head, I pictured Namiko's face and half-jokingly cursed her. Without her strategic networking, I wouldn't be flying toward Tibet, inching ever closer to the mythical mountain range where I was headed. But I also had her to thank for this shaky spin in a tin can with two guys afraid of mountain weather. She'd had to promise them extra payment to get them to agree to the trip at all.

That should have been my first red flag.

*I continue to be astounded by the miracle of human flight,* Marcus said, his voice full of wonder.

The plane bucked on a vicious air current. One of the pilots uttered something that sounded a hell of a lot like a curse. I swallowed the newest wave of nausea.

"That makes one of us," I muttered. "At least you're having fun."

*I have found that many potentially lethal experiences are much more enjoyable after death has already occurred,* he said cheerfully.

I took a deep breath to steady my nerves. "There's a sentence I never expected to hear."

It was hard to focus on Marcus's lighthearted banter.

Every creak from the airplane's metal body made me think of nuts and bolts raining down into the clouds while our structural integrity decreased by the minute. The thought that I might soon plummet to earth only heightened my urge to puke. I was fairly sure there'd be no river to cushion the impact this time, and no creepy smoking man to reorient me.

*Namiko was most generous to procure passage into the mountains.* Marcus blithely held up his end of the conversation, ignorant to the fact that we hurtled through a storm, probably surrounded by mountains, and that if we veered even slightly off course, we'd die in a fiery crash on the side of some lonely peak, never to be found.

"I wouldn't call it generous," I said, my teeth clenched. "I mean, okay, I would. In the sense that she didn't have to do it. But this wasn't what I had in mind when I asked."

The plane—which had listed at a sickening angle for at least five minutes—finally righted itself, and my whole body went limp from the release of massive tension. I flopped my head back on the headrest, my eyes still shut, and breathed a little easier.

Namiko had done her best in a bad situation. I knew that. I had arrived at her resistance base in the Bay Area after a few harrowing days of dodging Delano's minions as I worked my way west. I scrounged food wherever I could find it but otherwise, never left the truck. To stop driving meant to think about the situation in granular detail, so I only slept when I couldn't force my eyes to stay open any longer.

On some level, I couldn't afford to worry about what was going on at the temple or how long it would take me to get back. I simply didn't have the energy or the emotional fortitude to consider any of that, especially not Deacon.

I told myself over and over that he was fine, that they'd thrown him in some shitty jail cell so they could kill me in front of him later. It was still not the best reassurance but way better than the glaring alternative. The farther I drove, the more convinced I became that I was doing the right thing after all. I could either believe in my choices or fall into despair.

My self-distraction techniques worked well enough to carry me to the west coast without going insane, but not well enough to keep me from looking like shit warmed over on Namiko's doorstep. She'd opened the door, taken one look at me, and said, "Vic, come in before you die out there." She fed me a meal, gave me a room, and slowly coaxed the whole story out and unraveled the tangled threads of my narrative with the patience of a saint.

At the end of it all, she'd said, "Listen, I think Delano's beyond our capabilities here, but I'll see if we can't dispatch some people to the Midwest to keep the weaker minions out of your way. And I can get you to South Asia. I think."

"You're my fucking hero," I had said to her—before she booked my flights. The plane shuddered yet again, and I managed a strained laugh.

*I thought you were not having fun,* Marcus said.

"Does it look like I'm having fun?" I shook my head. "It's merely funny that I've spent months fighting a shitload of gods, narrowly escaped by the skin of my damn teeth, and now I'm about to die in the mountains. And it won't even be my own fault."

*You will be fine,* Marcus told me. *You have proven that it will take much more than inclement weather and a vehicle of dubious endurance to remove you from the earth.*

I chuckled. "I guess that's true. But wouldn't it be the ultimate burn on Delano if I survived his beating, only to be killed in a stupid plane crash? He'd be so mad."

*He would indeed be furious.* Marcus acknowledged. *The price for such a hollow victory, however—*

"I know, I know. I'm not hoping for it. I merely hate that guy so much."

*Evidence indicates that the feeling is mutual.*

The airplane continued to fight through the storm, and I continued to wish there was a barf bag somewhere nearby. Finally, the ride smoothed out a little and a wave of blinding light washed over us as we burst through the edge of the clouds. The pilots broke into a cheer of thankful relief. They signaled to me and pointed down toward a rocky, snowy landscape that gave way to broad fields before they spoke on their radios and we began our descent.

The narrow airstrip materialized out of what looked like a brown smudge in the field and I held my breath on the approach. It was nothing more than well-packed soil, and it looked slick. The landing gear dropped. The earth rushed up to meet us. I didn't breathe again until the aircraft touched down and jostled me against my seatbelt one last time.

"Holy shit," I said out loud. "We made it!"

*See? And you are no worse for wear.*

"That's debatable," I said.

The aircraft taxied to a stop at the end of the strip. I

undid my straps, opened the door, and almost fell out onto the side runner.

"Thank you!" I called to the pilots and waved. I had to hand it to those guys. As terrifying as that flight had been, they had pulled it off in the end.

They waved back, grinned, and shouted something in their native tongue. I retrieved the backpack I'd brought from Namiko's base, hefted it onto my shoulders, and jumped down to blessedly solid ground.

The field sprawled in all directions around me. In summer, it was likely lush and green, perhaps repurposed farmland. At the moment, it lay dormant under a patchy cover of snow, not unlike the land surrounding Delano's temple. The major differences were the mountains that rose up in the distance everywhere I looked.

*Onward!* Marcus proclaimed. *To the next stage of this new adventure.*

"Yeah." I walked away from the airstrip and adjusted my stride to compensate for the lingering ache in my leg. "Do you know what the craziest thing is?"

*What?*

I smiled grimly. "I think that was the easy part."

CHAPTER EIGHTEEN

I walked until the sun hung low in the sky and saw no signs of life except ruts in the dirt road that headed north from the airstrip. Back at Namiko's, I had done some research on the general area so was decently prepared for the enormous sense of isolation that weighed down on me as I traveled.

She had inspected the smoking man's tablet, declared it insufficient for my needs, and gave me a new GPS unit, which I consulted regularly. The tablet was still tucked away in an inside pocket of my coat. I had half a mind to throw it back at him the next time I saw him.

*This is a stark but beautiful country,* Marcus observed. *I myself have little personal experience with mountainous regions.*

"You're in luck," I said. "Something tells me we're about to get intimately familiar with this one."

If nothing else, we'd be stuck there until I managed to finagle a way home, but I pushed those worries aside. There was no sense in freaking out about that when we had only arrived. There was, apparently, business to handle first. I didn't know what that business was, but past experience had taught me that things tended to reveal themselves along the way. My job was to grin and bear it until that happened.

I continued along the dirt path, confident that at least the blinking indicator on my GPS led me in the right direction. The slope of the road began to climb. Most of me didn't have a problem with that, but it wasn't long before my bum leg put in a complaint.

"Damn that sword," I muttered and gritted my teeth against the dull, persistent pain.

*The* Gladius Solis *is a fearsomely effective weapon. It has served you well many a time.*

"Yeah, but it's not supposed to work *against* me," I replied. "That feels like a betrayal." I was quiet for a minute as I considered this. "I wonder if this is how Kronin felt when he died."

*Worse, perhaps. He knew that everything he had worked to build would be gone in that instant. We are fortunate to have been given another chance.*

I crested the top of the hill and looked out toward the craggy horizon. The road wound down until it disappeared from view as it stretched toward the base of the distant mountains. I sighed. "It's gonna be a long walk."

My eye caught a cluster of shapes huddled beside the road. A few dim lights flickered around them. "Hey, that looks like a village!" I double-checked my GPS, but the settlement was so small that I wasn't surprised it didn't show up on maps. Reinvigorated, I hurried toward the structures which appeared to have been constructed out of not much more than mud and stone.

*Incredible. From the miracle of flight to a primitive hovel in the space of an afternoon.*

"I'm so glad no one else can hear you right now," I said. "Don't talk shit about these guys. They might be our only help."

*I was merely commenting on the condition of their civilization,* Marcus replied, slightly huffy. *I agree that their knowledge may be indispensable.*

I rolled my eyes. "Then don't make this *weird.*" I smoothed my hair and straightened my clothes as I approached the boundary of the village. Most of the buildings appeared to be residential, at least to my uneducated eye. There were significantly more of them than I had first assumed, stacked on top of and directly adjacent to each other as they climbed a hillside. Up close, they were colorful, too, although the hues had been washed out by exposure to the elements. Rainbow strings of cloth flags fluttered over the main street.

"Whoa." I glanced around, wide-eyed. "This is pretty awesome, actually."

*It pales in comparison to the Roman Empire, of course.*

I frowned. "Let's find someone and hope they speak enough English to give us directions." The streets were cold and windswept but faces appeared in a few windows as I made my way deeper into the village. A door squeaked open on my left, and an old woman with a sweet, wrinkled face and a scarf tied around her head beckoned me inside. She placed her arm around my shoulders and urged me across the threshold.

"Thank you," I said, not at all sure that she understood. "Um, could you tell me how to find…" I retrieved the tablet and opened the map to show her. She blinked at the screen. "I'm looking for this mountain." I pointed at the dot on the map. "I really need to get there." The old lady turned her eyes to me. They were shiny and black and crinkled at the corners. "If you don't know, that's okay!"

She held up a slightly crooked finger, sat me down in one of the two chairs at her table, and hurried through a doorway. I opened my mouth to call after her but she had already gone. When she returned a minute later, she had a younger man with her, his face half obscured by a thick beard. She talked to him in what I thought might be the same language the pilots had spoken and gestured in my direction. I tried to look apologetic.

The man smiled. "Grandmother says you only speak English? She thinks that you are lost."

"Oh." I barely stopped myself from saying *shit* in time. "Well, she's two for two."

"I see." His smile widened. "How may I help you? This is a strange place to be lost in if you will allow me to say so."

I showed him the tablet. "Well, I need to get to this mountain and I'm not sure which one it is."

"It is true that there are many mountains in this region," he said a chuckled. "Let me see."

He took the device from my hand and studied it for a while with a slight frown. I thought I'd have to show him how to operate the touch screen, but he manipulated it without any problems.

"Ah," he said at last. "I understand. Unfortunately, this mountain is very far away. You are searching for a different village to the north. A few hundred miles."

I nodded and tried to conceal my disappointment. "All right. Thanks."

He handed back the tablet. "I am sorry that you have so far yet to go. Grandmother has taken a liking to you."

The old woman beamed and showed all her teeth.

"I appreciate the help," I said. "What's the quickest way to cover that kind of distance? I'm in a something of a rush."

He tilted his head to regard me curiously. "You are the only person I have ever met who rushes to the mountains." A thoughtful expression crossed his face. "But I may be able to help further." He retreated into the other room and returned wearing a parka. "There is a man in the village who owns a car. Perhaps he can take you the rest of the way." He said something to his grandmother, then opened the door and motioned for me to follow. "Come with me and we will ask him."

We went down the street and turned into an alley lined with doors and balconies so close that they almost touched. More flags hung between the railings amid empty clotheslines. The man knocked at the fourth door.

"We may have to try more than once," he told me. "Sometimes, he has trouble hearing."

The sound of shuffling footsteps reached our ears and a slot in the door opened. My guide spoke briefly. He pointed to me and I waved.

A second later, the door swung inward to reveal an older gentleman whose black hair had gone mostly grey. He inspected me closely. I showed him the tablet.

"Yes," he said. "I drive you."

"Really?" I couldn't keep the excitement out of my voice. Both men laughed.

"Yes, yes," said the driver. "We leave now. Road is empty at night." He motioned with his hands. "Faster."

"Okay," I said. "Awesome!" I turned to the first man. "Thank you so much. And thank your grandmother too." I checked my pockets. "I wish I had something to give you in exchange."

"Oh, no." The man shook his head. "You must not give me anything. Where you are going, you will need all you have." He smiled again and shook my hand. "Good luck to you, traveler. May you find the blessings you seek." He patted my shoulder and turned toward the old lady's house.

"Come, come," the driver said. He led me around the back of the building to a small, partially fenced lot. A car sat hidden under a thick tarp and I helped him unfasten the ties. It looked like an ancient cab, the yellow paint chipped and faded. The driver produced a key and unlocked my side before he hurried around the front hood to wedge himself behind the steering wheel. The interior smelled vaguely musty.

"Does it still run?" I joked before I realized that he might not know I was kidding.

To my great relief, he laughed. "It runs, yes! It runs." As a demonstration, he started the old engine, which coughed but rumbled to life. "See? Good car."

"Great car," I said.

He nodded. "Let's go."

We crept out of the lot at less than five miles an hour and gingerly negotiated the tight corners. But when we finally reached the actual road, he accelerated and the engine roared. The exhaust backfired a couple times. Villagers emerged from their houses and hung out the windows to watch us pass by. Some of them cheered.

"Do they know where we're going?" I asked.

The driver shrugged. "Probably no," he answered. "They simply wish you well."

We rode together in silence for a while as the old vehicle bumped over the unpaved road. Once the cab reached its optimum speed, it chugged along like an old, reliable workhorse. The driver glanced constantly at me in the rearview mirror. He seemed eager to socialize.

"What you are doing here?" he asked and seemed to choose his words carefully. "Vacation?"

I shook my head. "No vacation. I, uh…I heard this was a good place to come if you want to find yourself."

He grinned. "On top of mountain, find lots of cold, maybe. Snow and big sky. Storms."

I sat in silence and suppressed the instinctive response that those had better not be all there was. He frowned and his cheerful face darkened abruptly.

"It is dangerous," he told me. "Out here. There are a lot of bad things."

I raised an eyebrow. "Bad things, as in bad people? I can handle those."

"No." He wagged a finger in warning. "The evil ones, they walk amongst them."

I sighed. Exactly what I wanted to hear.

In the silence that ensued, I leaned back into the passenger seat and watched this new part of the world roll by. Every so often, the driver would gesture out one side of the car or the other to point out landmarks or try to share some interesting fact. I really wanted to ask him more about the aforementioned evil ones, but he didn't seem too keen on the subject. His eyes clouded over whenever he so much as started to mention them and I gave up after a while. The guy was doing me a huge favor. It would be stupid to antagonize him before he'd gotten me where I needed to go.

The hours ran into each other as we cruised down that lonely, winding road. The mountains inched closer and closer until I could no longer see the misty outlines of even the lowest peaks. Finally, we chugged our way into a proper little town with big old stones set into the roads.

The same densely packed, brightly colored houses lined the streets. Near the town center, an open-air market attracted decent crowds. I paused with my hand on the door. People walked the streets as I expected but there were all kinds of Forgotten, too. I identified satyrs, Weres, and a gaggle of the stunted golems we'd encountered in D.C. A tall, lean vampire in an elegant coat stood outside a pot maker's stall and examined the wares.

"What's going on here?" I mused.

The driver scowled for the first time since we'd left his home village. He spat out an ugly word that had to be a curse and accelerated away as soon as I shut the car door behind me. Lumbering, stone-skinned gargoyles ambled past, their chiseled features set to mild ambivalence. At first, I was tense and ready for imminent confrontation. But these streets were peaceful if not normal.

"This is weird," I muttered to Marcus. "Why don't they act like pricks?"

*They appear to lack the natural aggression we have observed thus far,* he responded. *I must confess, I have never seen it before.*

"Maybe they're under some kind of spell." I slipped as inconspicuously as possible through the streets and studied my surroundings as unobtrusively as I could. The satyrs there were sober, well-groomed, and unarmed. No one gave me a second glance. I entered the town bazaar and pretended to scan the stalls instead of their patrons. I was sure a fight would erupt at any moment.

Fortunately, that never happened. Humans and Forgotten browsed the handcrafted goods side by side. They made conversation. I felt like I had gone crazy.

"Hey! American girl!" An English-speaking voice cut through all the foreign buzz.

I turned to look at its source and saw a small, wiry man perched on a stool behind his stall. He motioned me over.

"A rare sight in these mountains," he said and laughed.

I made a vague gesture around the market. "What is all this?" I asked. "These people don't care about the..." I mimed horns, wings, and fangs.

He smiled. "Elsewhere, perhaps they are monsters, but not here. These have defied their former masters and freed their minds of oppression. They came in search of freedom, and that is what they found. We have simply accepted their presence."

"Huh." I took another look around the vicinity. "And it's working out."

He shrugged his thin shoulders. "So far. We know they could turn on us at any time. In the beginning, many of us lived in fear. But they never chose anything other than peace. Now, we believe they are no different from us in here." The shopkeeper tapped the left side of his chest.

I looked into the unwavering serenity of his eyes. "I wonder if this is the way it could be everywhere," I said quietly.

"Where are you from?" he asked.

"New York City."

He chuckled. "And you do not have stranger citizens than this in New York?" He nodded his head at a small herd of centaurs that trotted down the middle of the road. They moved slowly so as not to pose a danger to the surrounding pedestrians and smiled as they greeted humans and other Forgotten alike. The brands on their bodies had faded to almost nothing.

I still had trouble wrapping my mind around the concept of humans and Forgotten coexisting. "Do you know where to find a guide?" I asked. "I'd like to go into the mountains."

"Ah," he said. "So that is your business." He leaned out of the stall and pointed down to the end of the row of buildings, immediately beyond the far perimeter of the market. "There, you will find your guide."

"Thanks." I moved quickly toward the house. Now that I was hyperaware of the Forgotten that roamed the street, it was a little unsettling to be outside. I ducked into the side alley and knocked on the door.

*What an extraordinary place,* said Marcus. I was certain that he said that with a frown. *I am not sure how I feel.*

"You and me both, my friend." On the surface, this town looked like a utopia, and maybe it really was. But it sure felt as weird as hell.

The person who answered the door was a kid, shorter than me with a mop of dark hair that hung in his big brown eyes. He could not have been more than sixteen or seventeen. "What's wrong?" he asked me in English. "Do you need help?"

"Uh." I hesitated. "Someone told me I'd be able to find a guide at this house. I'm sorry if I have the wrong address." I took out the tablet to show him.

"No, you are correct," the boy said. "I would be happy to guide you."

"You're the guide?" The question popped out of my mouth before I had the chance to stop it.

He nodded as if it was the most natural thing in the world. "Do not be worried. I am young but the mountains favor me. We will have no trouble."

*This child is either very brave or very stupid.*

I tried to look past him into the house in case there were any adults around. "Are you absolutely sure about that?" I asked.

"Yes, yes." He stepped aside to let me in. "I have guided many feet to the peaks and down. I promise you, this is the truth." He smiled. "Take a room in the house for your rest tonight. Tomorrow, we leave at daybreak." He closed the door.

I stood there in the dim, narrow hall for a minute or two and mulled over this new situation. The kid didn't move and he didn't stop smiling either. "All right," I said. There was nothing to do but press forward. "We leave at daybreak."

## CHAPTER NINETEEN

A brisk tap on my bedroom door woke me from a dead sleep the next morning. The kid was there, bright-eyed and bushy-tailed and all geared up for our expedition. His pack was at least as big as the one I'd brought with me, and he still grabbed mine and slung it on his back.

"Hey, I can carry that," I said as I rubbed the sleep from my eyes.

"Nope," was his only reply. He ran to the other room and returned with some breakfast in the form of bread, water, and dried meat, which he pressed into my hand. "Eat. We have to go. The climb is half a day's journey and we do not want to come down in the dark."

I decided not to mention the fact that I had no idea what was in store up there or if I'd even come down at all. Instead, I stuffed some jerky in my face and trailed down the hall after him, out of the house, and into the still-dark street.

The first misty fingers of morning had barely pushed

up from the horizon, and the air was bitterly cold. The kid's trajectory was set and sure. He trotted to the town center, where the empty skeleton of the bazaar waited to fill up for the day. A few young men stood around with rickshaws and rubbed their hands together. The boy picked one and hopped on. I joined him.

The two of them talked for a while on the way out of town. I sat in the back with my hands in my lap and felt strangely unencumbered without my pack. My young guide, on the other hand, looked like he shouldn't have been able to move under all that weight, but he was as hardy as a goat. The rickshaw operator dropped us off at a trailhead in the steeper foothills, and the kid walked unbowed ahead of me, his hair blowing in the wind. My leg protested but I picked up my pace to draw even with him.

"You are limping," he observed. "Would you like to return to the town?"

I waved away his concern. "It's nothing," I said. "I'll be fine. I've looked forward to this hike for weeks." It was something of an exaggeration but not wholly untrue. I *did* want to know what waited at the summit of this mountain. Also, I wanted this trip over with so I could head back to Indiana as soon as possible. Delano wouldn't wait around and look for me forever.

"Let me know if you change your mind." Those eight words were the most the boy spoke aloud for a long time.

He traversed the trail effortlessly and his expression never deviated from one of simple calm. I realized that he was at home up there, even loaded down with two packs and thick, insulated clothing. I wondered if he liked it better at higher altitudes because of all the Forgotten in his town.

It was tough to simply dive into that kind of heavy discourse so I decided to start small. "Hey, I never got your name," I said. "I'm Vic."

He gave me a slight smile. "My name is Shiva," he said.

I grinned back. "Oh yeah? How does it feel to be named after a god these days?"

Shiva knitted his brows. "I am named for a real god," he replied. "Not like these imposters."

*Ha! The unadulterated wisdom of youth.*

"My guess is you're not the biggest fan of all those 'imposters' living around your home then," I said.

To that, he shook his head and his shaggy hair swung back and forth over his eyes. "Those creatures are not the same," he answered. "My people are much more open-minded to certain things than your cultures in the West. We know those beings are not evil, and we have learned to reside together in harmony. This has happened for months." He adjusted the double pack on his shoulder without slowing down. "They have given us nothing to fear."

Marcus grumbled. *I rescind some of my previous statement. The Forgotten have never been anything but trouble. It is folly for this boy and his people to allow them space in their town.*

I wanted to respond but it became more difficult. The wound in my leg carried a persistent, painful beat that strengthened the more time I spent walking. Tiny beads of sweat formed on my skin, aftereffects of powering through the pain. Still, I pushed onward.

Shiva pulled a little ahead again and I clenched my jaw

in determination. I told myself that a half day's climb was nothing and that I'd rest at the summit in no time.

For a while, that tactic worked. I was able to put my injury out of my thoughts and focus on the austere beauty of the mountains. When the grades became steeper, though, my leg complained louder as I scrambled up nearly vertical faces and squeezed through tall, narrow crevices. The discomfort gradually worked its way up to my hip and engulfed most of the right side of my body. A few times, I paused instinctively for tiny respites when Shiva wasn't looking but stopping wasn't an option, no matter how hard this damn mountain kicked my ass. I had already screwed up once. I wouldn't do it again.

Mother Nature, however, had other plans. The clear sky we had enjoyed since dawn was rapidly smothered by the same heavy grey clouds my plane had flown through on the way into this region of South Asia. The change in weather gave Shiva pause. He studied the patterns in the cloud cover and finally said, "It would be wise to turn back now. This is not good climbing weather. It is no longer safe."

I stopped beside him and turned my gaze to the unfriendly sky. "I don't doubt you," I said. "You're the guide here. But I need to keep going." I glanced at his clean-shaven teenage face. "If you're afraid, it's okay. I won't judge you. I've been scared too. But if your concern is for me, it's not necessary."

Shiva chewed his lip. "I am not fearful," he admitted. "There was a time once, when I was a child, that I was stranded by a storm in the mountains for four days. My survival made me believe that my time is appointed by higher beings. It will come when it comes, whether that is on this peak or on the rickshaw going home." Despite this brave talk, the uneasiness refused to leave his face. He stood with his feet planted firmly and stared at the rest of the mountain path.

I laughed. "Don't sweat it, kid. I've spent the better part of a year constantly on the edge and waiting to be dropped into the great abyss. If I can hang on for this long, so can you. Let's keep going, okay? You and me. I'll be with you all the way."

"You had better be," Shiva said. "For your own sake." He moved forward again and guided me along increasingly narrow switchbacks into a hovering blanket of fog. The freezing water droplets clung to my face and eyelashes and blurred my vision. My whole leg ached fiercely. Shiva was little more than two vague backpack humps ahead of me. I pushed to keep up because to lose sight of him meant sheer catastrophe.

This high up, the rocks were frigid and slick. I climbed with my heart in my throat and fought to ignore the incredible altitude. My hands and feet slid on the icy surfaces, and more than once, I felt myself lose all purchase for half a terrifying second. And man, did my leg hurt.

I hadn't had more than a passing chance to rest it since I'd left San Francisco, and that now caught up with me. It was almost all I could do to stay on Shiva's tail. He might as well have been an apparition for all I could of see him through the mist.

Then, I saw his partial silhouette falter. One foot slipped free of the ledge he walked on and I stared in horror as he slid toward the edge of a deep, dark crevasse.

The opening was narrow but not narrow enough to keep him from falling to his death. Shiva shouted something that was whipped away by the wind.

All thoughts of my personal safety left my mind. I shoved myself off the rock with all my might and hurtled toward his falling form. His right hand grasped desperately for any hold but found nothing. He had only yards before he was lost forever.

I ran on my sore, unsteady leg as far as I could along that rickety ledge. My footing slipped too, but I used that to my advantage and dived down toward Shiva.

"Grab my hand!" I yelled.

He looked up as I seized his fingers. The jerk as his momentum halted almost tore me loose from the precarious hold I had on the cliff face. Thankfully, I managed to hold on, even if only barely, and I used my good leg to drag us both back to relative safety. We slumped side by side against the rock, our mirrored pants testimony to shared relief. My heart thrummed wildly in my chest.

"How can you be so strong?" he asked somewhat reverently. "Never mind. I do not question. I am only grateful."

"I go to the gym," I told him. "Like, a lot."

*You were also trained by a brilliant, dashing centurion of the Roman army*, Marcus piped up. *His words instilled you with the courage you now selflessly exhibit on a regular basis. You can only hope to one day be molded in his noble image.*

I sucked in a deep breath and let it out. "Yep," I said. "Definitely the gym."

## CHAPTER TWENTY

We slowed our pace after that little mishap and picked our way cautiously through the thin, wet air. The rocks grew a covering of ice and then snow. By the time we reached the path to the summit, we trudged through it, paranoid at the thought of hidden ravines. Shiva pulled himself up over a ledge and stopped to catch his breath. He pointed straight ahead.

"The peak," he said. "It's there. A hundred feet."

I perched beside him and surreptitiously massaged my leg. "Thank you, Shiva. You can turn back now. I'll take it from here."

"What do you mean?" He gazed at me with a trace of suspicion. "You must not believe you can make the descent without a guide. Climbing down is harder, not easier. You cannot see where you are going." He sounded a little irritated as if I wasn't the first dumb foreigner to try to dismiss him early. Unlike the others before me, I wouldn't be dissuaded.

"You talked about your appointed time before," I said

and scowled at the swirl of fog and snow above. "This is mine. I have to meet it alone." Talking to him that way gave me flashbacks of when I'd said more or less the same thing to my crew at the base of Delano's temple. I hoped dearly that this venture, whatever it turned out to be, would have a happier ending.

Shiva surprised me by moving to block the path. His eyes were somber. "You tricked me," he said. "Had I known you meant to end your life here, I would not have agreed to be your guide."

I gasped. "No! No, no, kiddo. I'm not here for that. That's insane."

"Is it?" he demanded. "I have seen it happen many times. Lost souls find their way to the peaks so that their last moments may pass as close to paradise as they can be. They believe it will make the transition easier. Less painful? More peaceful? I do not know." He shook his head to clear it. "I cannot allow you to die this way, whether or not it is your wish."

"Shiva, listen to me." I grabbed the kid's gloved hand in my own. "I didn't climb all this way to die on the summit. I don't want to meet the gods. I want to know how to kill them."

The poor boy understood that even less, judging by the way he stared at me like I'd grown another head. He looked like he debated whether to drag my crazy ass back down to the town anyway, but at the last moment, he thought better of it.

"You are not suffering from oxygen deprivation," he said as though he needed to convince himself.

"No," I insisted. "I know what I'm here to do, and I want

you to know you can't stop me. Go home, Shiva. I'll see you when I see you. Don't forget that you're not responsible for the choices I've made."

He wanted very badly to argue and to talk me out of it. I could see it in his face, and I really felt for him. To someone who lacked the context for everything I had said, I was sure I sounded insane—and yes, like a person with a weird death wish.

*Here lies Vic, the woman who wanted to kill the gods.*

But he saw through to my grim conviction and backed away reluctantly before he turned in the direction from which we'd come a few minutes earlier. I watched until I was absolutely certain that he hadn't doubled back and I set out for the peak.

The last hundred feet were brutal in a way I never expected. I clawed my way up the practically sheer face, one slip away from certain doom. My feet scrabbled against slippery rock and snow fell away on either side to plummet thousands of feet to a bottom beyond my imagination. The sound of my heart pounded in my head. With every shallow breath, I inched a little higher.

Near the very top, the whine of the sharp wind rose to a screech. The currents of air ripped at my body and threatened to tear me off the mountain and throw me into a hidden grave. A couple of times, I stopped moving entirely and clung to the rocks until I stopped shaking. "Fucking hell," I whispered hoarsely. "If I ever see that smoking jackass again, I'm gonna punch him in the face. I don't care what's up here."

*Focus, Victoria. You are very close.*

"Yeah, yeah." I scrabbled above me with my right hand

and hooked my fingers over a reasonably flat edge that felt deeper than a few inches. My heart skipped a beat. I grabbed hold with my other hand, and for a second, I swung freely from the shoulders down. The excitement drowned out the fear as I hauled myself up over the ledge and onto the peak of my mountain. Nothing but a slate-grey sky loomed over my head.

I almost cried with relief and joy but my rest only lasted a minute. Soon, I pushed to my feet and walked forward while I searched for clues. The fog was thicker than ever up there, but there was no hiding the massive, ornately carved wooden door fitted into the mountain's highest point. It was ancient and smooth and there was something strangely familiar about its design.

"Ready?" I asked Marcus. My hand touched the wood.

*As ever, Victoria. Let us away.*

I exhaled a billowing plume of white and I pushed firmly against it.

The door rumbled open, and I walked through.

## CHAPTER TWENTY-ONE

On the other side of the door, the howling wind was immediately silenced. The bone-chilling cold melted into soothing heat. The mountain peak was replaced by a vast banquet room with a golden throne. Lavish trappings notwithstanding, the room lay empty and still but my eyes were drawn to something other than the inexplicable finery. Standing off to my left was a person I hadn't seen in a small eternity. My mouth dropped open. "Marcus?"

He grinned broadly and stepped forward with his arms out. "Hail, Victoria."

"You son of a bitch!" I said and hugged him tightly. "What the hell?"

He laughed and returned the embrace. "It is wonderful to truly see you again, my friend. And to occupy the same physical space."

We looked at each other for a long time and I soaked in the bizarre reality of the moment.

"Seriously, what the hell?" I asked. "Five seconds ago, I

was climbing a mountain and you were right here." I patted the medallion which still hung around my neck. Its metal was no longer warm to the touch and it had lost some of its ethereal luster. "Now, we're in a fucking throne room and you're in front of me. In the flesh." The words were surreal to my ears.

"Calm yourself, Victoria." Marcus chuckled and rested a hand on my shoulder. "What else would you expect from the realm of the gods?"

"The realm of the—" I jerked backward to study the rich chamber one more time. "You have got to be shitting me."

He made a face. "I am not, in fact, doing that." He turned and spread his arms wide in a gesture he had probably practiced since the dawn of time. "Welcome to Carcerum."

"Damn." I couldn't keep the goofy smile off my face. "I gotta be honest. I never thought I'd be so happy to see your ugly mug."

Marcus didn't answer right away and I was about to rib him again when I noticed his attention had become fixed on something across the room. I pivoted, and my exuberant grin instantly faded. The smoking man sat upon the golden throne, his legs crossed casually and a cigarette clamped between his lips. Immediately, I looked toward Marcus to gauge his reaction. The old centurion was so guarded, he revealed nothing.

I knew what I wanted to say, but I kept it locked tightly behind my teeth. What the shit was *that* guy doing there? My fists clenched instinctively at my sides. I still wanted to throw that punch for everything he'd put me through.

The man watched us impassively as he took another deep drag. "Come," he instructed, his head wreathed in a white plume.

As if compelled by an outside force, Marcus and I stepped forward in unison until we stood below the steps that led to the throne. The smoking man uncrossed his legs. He stubbed his cigarette out in a jeweled ashtray and its miniscule embers faded into nothing. Then, he stood and something happened to the sinewy old-man body. He grew and his shoulders broadened. His jawline became clean and sharp. The shape of his muscles filled out. He even glowed a little.

I blinked. The smoking man had gone, replaced by a man who could only be a king. Although his face was drawn with hidden pain, his features looked like they'd been sculpted by an artist and he exuded an irresistible charisma.

Marcus gasped. When I glanced his way, he had dropped to one knee, his head bowed in utmost reverence. "My Lord," he intoned.

I folded my arms. "My Lord is right," I said. "Will somebody tell me what in high freaking heaven is going on here?"

The old centurion looked aghast at my impropriety. "Victoria!" he chastised. "That is no way to speak before the God-King. I will thank you to show the proper respect in his hall."

I gave him a hard look. "Dude, listen to yourself right now. The God-King's gone, and it's a damn good thing he is because Delano beat me up and took his sword—or don't you remember that part? Something tells me he wouldn't be too happy if he knew."

Marcus grimaced. He obviously wanted to shrivel up and die of embarrassment. "Victoria—"

"Well, she's not completely wrong." The man spoke for the first time since his transformation. "I must admit, I was disheartened to witness that particular defeat. But the fault lies with me, Vic. Not you."

I stopped cold. My eyes locked onto his face and revelation crashed over me. "Tell me who you are," I said. "Uh…please."

Marcus sighed audibly.

The man only smiled. "My name is nothing you don't already know," he replied. "I am Kronin, former king of the gods, ruler of Carcerum, and bearer of the *Gladius Solis*. Loyal Marcus speaks the truth. You walk in my domain."

## CHAPTER TWENTY-TWO

My jaw dropped as the force of the truth smacked me in the face. The smoking man, the guy who fished me out of an Indiana river after he'd left me and my crew to fend for ourselves against Delano, had been Kronin the whole time.

Memories of his brief appearances during the last months of my life flashed through my head. They all had one thing in common—he showed up, dispensed some sage wisdom, and dropped off the face of the earth again, often for weeks without any form of contact. Knowing that he had likely retreated to his undisturbed godly kingdom during those periods of strife made me mad. Then I thought about it some more and it made me furious.

Marcus must have seen the color rise in my face because he reached out a hand toward my arm, ready to mediate between me and his lord and savior.

Steaming, I brushed him off. "You have some nerve, Kronin," I said. "You know that? Leave it to one of the freaking gods to let the world fall into chaos while they sit idly by, doing nothing." I glared directly into his eyes and refused to give an inch. He made no reply. "And now you have nothing to say. Typical."

The centurion's hand landed on my shoulder. He tried to ease me back gently, maybe because he was afraid I'd storm up those fancy golden steps and slap the God-King in his omniscient face. His grip was firm but I didn't budge. My hurt leg trembled slightly and I prayed it wouldn't give out. Marcus made another attempt to mollify me.

"Keep your temper," he said softly. "We need Kronin now more than ever."

I had already seen red, however. "No," I retorted and continued to glower at the king of gods. "We don't. The only thing he's done for us is make false promises." I could literally feel my blood pressure rise and a tension headache brewed in the back of my skull.

The fact that Kronin had yet to go on the defensive only annoyed me more. There was no honor in simply sitting there and taking it. I was more than happy to force him into a direct confrontation and release some of the pent-up frustration. Maybe after that, I'd be able to look at him without wanting to throw up.

"You—" I didn't really know what I wanted up to say, but as it turned out, it didn't matter. My voice had risen to a level barely below a shout, and when I went to kick it up a notch, my lungs refused to cooperate. Instead of taking a stand, I doubled over and coughed so hard that I eventually sagged onto the floor. Marcus knelt at my side and glanced at Kronin.

"I must apologize for her, my liege. She is very weak and she is not herself. I am sure you understand that these past weeks have been exceptionally difficult for her on many levels. But she is strong. She will recover."

I swatted at him and did my best to indicate that his sentiments were full of crap and he didn't have permission to speak for me. Recent events had been as tough as hell, but so was I.

"I'm not weak," I tried to say. "I'm fucking pissed." The cough wouldn't abate, however, and the words were reduced to a series of rusty croaks. Not cool or impressive, I acknowledged miserably.

"Relax, Vic." Kronin broke his contemplative silence at last. "I mean that literally. Nourish your body with food, drink, and rest. Hospitality is the least I can provide you in the wake of a journey like the one you've had. The halls of Carcerum will no doubt refresh you as they have rejuvenated me on countless occasions. It is an honor to host you."

Marcus helped me up and slung my arm around his shoulders. I mumbled a sullen reply.

"Thank you, my Lord," Marcus said. "We are most grateful."

Kronin nodded. He addressed me again. "Once your strength has returned, I shall answer for every choice I have made thus far—the good and the bad. You may judge me then as you see fit." He stepped back and resumed his position on the gleaming throne. Marcus bowed his head and guided me toward an archway at the end of the hall.

"Where are we going?" I rasped. "I'm not done with him yet."

"It can wait," Marcus replied, a touch of dry amusement in his tone. "For now, Kronin is right. You need to recuperate and get strong. Time flows differently in Carcerum, but it does not stop."

He walked me carefully through shining corridors to a luxurious bedchamber. While I dragged myself under the downy covers, the old Roman soldier brought me strange, brightly colored fruits that dripped with sweet juice, water clearer than crystal, and a ladle brimful of the mystical nectar that worked overtime to keep me alive.

I didn't think I was hungry until he piled food on plates in front of me, balanced across the bedspread on a polished tray. Once I'd lifted the first piece of exotic fruit to my lips, I recalled suddenly that I hadn't had anything to eat since my breakfast of bread and jerky at Shiva's house. Marcus sat on the end of the bed, watched me devour his offerings, and smiled like a proud dad.

"You eat like a true warrior," he said.

I licked juice off my fingertips. "At least I do something like a damn warrior." Under the comforter, I stretched my bad leg out in search of a comfortable position. The pain had eased but it did not disappear. "I'm about to sleep like one. That's for sure."

"A hero's rest," Marcus affirmed. He cleared the empty plates away and ran a cloth over the tray. The ladle of nectar was refilled.

"I feel bad watching you act like my butler," I confessed and took a long draught of nectar. "Don't get me wrong. It's also amazing. But I can't help thinking it's, like, a step down for you."

The soldier laughed. He turned down the edges of the blankets and tucked them in around me. "It is no matter. To have a corporeal form at all is an occasion to be savored. I would be grateful to do anything with these hands."

I gazed at him. "I can't believe it. I mean, I'm really, really glad to see you but I didn't know this was possible." I paused. "How *is* it possible? I thought bringing back the dead was usually number one on the list of things that are never allowed."

Marcus shrugged his shoulders. "No more than the miracle of Carcerum," he answered. "I am grateful that you are allowed to experience it in all its glory." A shadow crossed his face. "Well, some of its glory. It wasn't always quite so…hollow."

I shuffled down into the bed and sighed as the luxurious mattress hugged my exhausted body. "I want to ask you something, and I need you to be a hundred percent honest with me," I said. "No, more than that. Like a thousand percent."

My eyelids instantly became heavy. I stifled a yawn. The million thoughts in my head slowed to a crawl.

"I have never been anything but honest with you, my friend," said Marcus. "This will always be true."

"Good." I rolled onto my side and faced him. "Do you know what's going on here, for real?"

He shook his head. "We are in the same boat, Victoria. My guess is as valuable as yours." His eyes moved toward the half-draped window that caught the light. "But one thing I do know above all else is that if Kronin is alive, all will be well. I feel it in my very soul. He has not forsaken us."

"Hmm." I blinked slowly and fought the powerful force that drew me into sleep. "I'm not so sure about that."

Marcus touched my arm. "Have faith, Victoria, and hope. Sometimes, in the darkest hours, these are what carry us through."

His words followed me down into a dreamless dark. They made me think of Deacon in the moments before I drifted off. If only faith, hope, and love could be enough.

## CHAPTER TWENTY-THREE

C ocooned in the finest, softest blankets I had ever felt, I slept for what might have been hours or days or weeks. All I knew when I woke up was that it was the most fulfilling rest I'd had in a long, long time. The feeling reminded me a little of life before the gods and waking up to go to work, or practice, or college classes.

Except I now woke up in Carcerum on the other side of the veil from the Himalayan Mountains. Someone had come in while I slept and dropped breakfast off on that same polished tray. I dug in and relished the sensation of being full of rich, nutritious food. Months of stews and preserved rations had dulled my taste buds, but they wasted no time and seemed to spring immediately back to life.

I leaned back on the pillows for a moment after my meal and absorbed the abundance of comfort. No wonder Marcus could never shut up about the place.

The bedroom had an adjoining bath. In my haste to fall asleep as quickly as possible, I had not used it. Now, I stood on the bath mat, stripped off my dirty, travel-worn clothes, and dropped them onto the pristine floor. The soles of my feet left smears in the basin of the tub, even though I'd worn boots on my way up the mountain. I twisted the knobs on either side of the faucet and realized they were golden. Everything here was golden.

Steam curled from the water as it swirled around my feet. I basked in the heat, my eyes closed, and grinned. I couldn't remember the last time I'd been so pampered—or had the time and facilities to soak in a bathtub. My worries and fears washed away with the grime on my skin. For the moment, I felt free.

I lingered there, submerged up to my neck, until the water was gross and dingy. Then, I drained it, filled it again, and washed myself totally clean. As I lathered soap along my legs, I took a minute to inspect my sword wound closely for the first time since I'd received it. There was no more blood but it didn't look healed, either. The skin around the incision was dark. I touched it lightly, winced, and jerked my hand back.

"Yep," I muttered. "It still hurts." But it was better. I could stand and walk without too much of a problem. I had dealt with far worse than occasional shooting pains.

The towels were huge and fluffy and seemed to drink the moisture right off my skin. I found a comb and ran it through my hair. The mirror told me that the dark circles under my eyes had finally decided to vacate the premises. To be honest, I didn't look half bad. Of course, the one day I looked super good, Deacon wasn't there to appreciate it.

The simple act of thinking about him made my stomach squeeze uncomfortably. I finished getting dressed and left the bedchamber for a self-guided tour around Carcerum. The inside of my head remained amazingly quiet as I headed down the hall. It was almost weird not to have Marcus constantly chatting away in there. Still, I wasn't about to take total independence for granted.

Beyond Kronin's combination banquet hall and throne room, I found an atrium that opened into the wildest gardens I had ever seen. I took a peek at the throne as I passed. It stood empty and so did the hall before it. The fragrance of flowers struck my senses as I passed beneath a glass dome that filtered sunlight down to hundreds of multicolored blooms. The garden air was sweet and heavy. It was tempting to sit on one of the ornate benches along the path, but I walked on through a door on the other side of the glass-walled greenhouse. A whole world stretched beyond the confines of the palace, and I wanted to see as much of it as possible.

The land was gorgeous and sweeping, painted in every shade imaginable—plus some I swore I'd never seen. Every blade of grass, every drop of water, and every pebble beside the immaculate roads held a muted glow in its depths. The soaring sky blazed cerulean above my head. The sun followed wherever I went and caressed my skin with its subtle warmth. Winter was nonexistent in Carcerum and I didn't miss it all that much.

I strolled along the footpaths that threaded through the kingdom until my leg began to act up a little. It was a simple matter to find my way back. I simply needed to check the horizon for the imperial outline of Kronin's palace. I chose a straight path toward it and approached the grounds from a different angle to which I had left them. I ended up in a smaller set of outdoor gardens artfully arranged around the base of a burbling fountain.

Kronin sat on the side of the fountain's basin—smoking, as usual. He gazed into the rippling water, deep in rumination. I slowed my pace. Food and sleep had cooled a lot of the searing anger I'd unleashed upon my arrival in Carcerum, and although I still had some burning questions for the guy, I harbored a pang of remorse for my actions.

"Good morning," Kronin said suddenly. He glanced at me and smiled. "You're feeling well, I hope." If he thought I was an asshole for shouting at him, his grace never faltered.

"Yeah," I said sheepishly. "Much better. Listen, I'm sorry for acting like a prick—like a jerk—when I got here. I won't take back what I said, but I realize I could have said it better." I scratched my head. "I was in a bad way. I guess you could probably tell."

He studied me quietly. "There is no need to apologize," he said. "Your anger is justified. There are many things that I would perhaps change if I had the opportunity. But the past is untouchable, and so we must look to the future instead." He stood. "Please, walk with me. I want to show you the kingdom."

We walked the land in silence for a while, side by side as we took in the immeasurable majesty of the realm. Experiencing it with Kronin was a far different experience than it had been on my own. Miles seemed to slip by in minutes. We followed a path down to a point that overlooked a grand, sprawling city. The maze of streets lay below us, eerily devoid of life. Then, he led me in another direction through thick forests and rolling fields. Small, cozy hamlets dotted the countryside. These, too, were empty. I quickly lost count of the places we saw, and each one stood abandoned, waiting patiently for anyone to return.

"This place," Kronin said as he stared out into the distance, "was once inhabited by beings much greater than the gods. They were the creators of all that we know today —the Earth, the gods themselves, even humanity. As you can see, they are long gone. They were gone even when I first arrived. Carcerum was empty then, the same way it is now."

"Where did they go?" I asked.

"That is an excellent question." He stopped to consider it and tilted his head back. The sunlight poured across his face to highlight his impeccable features. "Maybe they grew bored with their little pet project on your planet and left it behind for other, more interesting pursuits. Or they could have died, I suppose, assuming they had natural lifespans. It's impossible to know." He continued his walk without elaborating. I found his habitual vagueness annoying.

"Speaking of death," I said pointedly, "I thought *you* were dead. And so did Marcus."

The God-King's smile was grim this time, and sad. "I am not dead," he answered. "But I am dying. Delayed as its effects may be, the blow that Lorcan dealt was still a fatal one. I have survived this long thanks only to the sustaining power of this wonderful place. If not for my necessary forays down to your realm, I could have lived longer." He shook his head. "It is not to be. The thread of my existence frays thinner as we speak. The nectar and the herbs can only do so much."

I smirked. "I wondered how you could stand to chain-smoke like that."

Kronin chuckled. "Yes. In fact, the smoking is what lent me so much borrowed time. The element of disguise was simply a necessary side benefit. To reveal my true identity would have been to invite an even more powerful danger upon the world. The gods' efforts to end me once and for all would have reduced the human realm to dust."

I chewed my lip. "Why did you do it, Kronin? It seems…" I didn't finish the sentence.

"Stupid?" he suggested. "Naïve? Foolhardy? Perhaps it was all of those things. I wanted to ensure that the sword fell into the right hands." He looked at me. "I believe that particular mission has been accomplished. You still have the raw strength to triumph over Delano's plague of evil."

"I used to think that," I said. "Then he trounced me, and now, I'm not positive anymore. I know I need to go back but it might not be enough."

"I doubted myself once, too," Kronin said.

Our route meandered in a wide, lazy circle around the palace. No matter where I looked, the scene was utterly breathtaking. Sparkling waterfalls cascaded over violet, clean-cut cliffs. Verdant forests swayed in a gentle, floral-scented breeze. Birdsong floated past my ears. I had always thought Marcus was pretty full of it, the way he went on and on about Carcerum. Now that I knew it was every bit as idyllic as he'd said, a seed of resentment began to fester.

"Why the heck did you bring the gods to this place?" I demanded. We now angled gradually back toward the palace grounds. Immediately outside the garden perimeter, Marcus appeared and fell into step beside us. I spoke again, unable to suppress my irritation. "The way they whined about it, I pictured a prison." I scoffed. "It turns out it's more like a paradise. Too good for them." It pissed me off to imagine scum like Lorcan being allowed to exist in this beautiful realm. He never deserved to look at it, much less live in it.

"I had no choice," Kronin told me sadly. "Without Lorcan's help, I could never have defeated the other gods and won the war in the first place. We both knew that, and so we made a deal. The gods were granted life in Carcerum in lieu of death on Earth. I thought it was a good bargain, one that they would accept, if not embrace." He pressed his lips together. "Obviously, I was mistaken."

Marcus looked pained but he remained silent. Kronin went on. "I believed with all my heart that I would be able to give the gods everything they wanted, everything to keep them happy. I failed to understand that they didn't want to be happy. They wanted control. Lorcan had known that all along. He'd planned, bided his time, and Delano never wavered from his side."

"Hold on." I held up my hand. "I still don't understand why you had to make a deal with that idiot in the first place. You're Kronin the Almighty, wielder of the *Gladius Solis*. The original God-King. Why bother making deals with Lorcan or anyone else?"

"What else was I to do?" he countered. "I am only human, after all."

## CHAPTER TWENTY-FOUR

Marcus and I both halted abruptly and stared dumbstruck at Kronin's back.

"Human?" Marcus murmured, disbelieving.

Kronin nodded. "I had a family, once upon a time," he said. "A lovely wife and sweet, innocent children. We lived in a house on the outskirts of a little village. I ran a forge and made pots and horseshoes and other useful things. It was a good and simple life, and yet I still allowed myself to be pressured by a god into leaving it behind." His face darkened briefly. "The god's name has long since been lost in the annals of history—that's how inconsequential he was in the end. Nonetheless, I knew no better. I packed my things up and rode out to battle in service of this tiny deity. I witnessed many horrors then, but none compared to what I found upon my return."

"Oh, no," I said softly.

"The gods were gone from my village," Kronin said. "Who knows if they even made it there. It was their creatures who found and destroyed it. They burned the houses down and reduced everything to broken piles of rubble. I rode as fast as I could, hoping against hope that they might have turned back before they reached my home." He shook his head and kept it lowered. "My wife, my children—they weren't spared. In my grief, I made a furious vow to cleanse the world of these murdering vermin. I wanted to make sure they were indeed forgotten. I merely didn't know how to make it happen."

"My liege." Marcus's voice was full of sorrow. "I had no idea."

Kronin continued his story, seemingly heedless of any interruption. The sentences poured out of him as if they'd been held hostage behind a dam for centuries. "I gave up everything I knew to travel the world in search of any scrap of information that could help me bring about their demise. I wanted a mass Forgotten extinction. No lead was too small, too strange, or too insignificant. I began to push the boundaries of human experience. This is what led me eventually to Carcerum." He paused. "And Carcerum, in turn, gave me its two greatest treasures—the nectar and the Solis Stone. One granted me life from a well I perceived to be limitless. The other allowed me to forge a weapon like none other. An inimitable sword which carried in its blade the power to slay the beasts that had torn my world asunder—and the gods who had shaped their existence."

Kronin shook his head. "With my gifts in hand, I returned to humankind and convinced them to rally behind my godlike strength. We rose up as one, millions strong, to fight back against the invasion. The war reached a fever pitch. Our clashes with the gods were brutal and bloody. Human life was lost in droves." He gazed at his hands and his voice lowered. "I came to realize the sword alone was not enough, and neither was my iron will. The army I had amassed was no match for the gods and their Apprenti. They were too formidable, and we were severely outnumbered. Every victory of ours came with a dozen setbacks. The gods constantly replenished their forces. I thought the war would rage forever until the Earth was nothing but a dead husk of a planet.

"Then, an emissary arrived in our midst. His name was Delano, and he had been sent by his master Lorcan, a death god. The offer he presented was undeniable. If I had dared refuse, all of humanity would have been extinguished. It was only a matter of time." He rubbed a hand across his face. The lustrous color in his skin had started to fade slightly. "The deal was struck. The war ended and I brought the gods here to Carcerum." His mouth turned down into the shadow of a scowl. "We left the other riffraff behind. The threat of serving time in Asphodel was enough to force them into hiding their true natures. And that was how we kept the balance for thousands of years."

"Wow." I whistled. I had no idea what else to say.

Kronin walked a few more yards and sat heavily on a bench. He was definitely paler and his fingers fumbled slightly as he withdrew a cigarette. He lit it, leaned back, and dragged on it. "I need not say again that my days are numbered," he said. "I am sorry that I won't be able to finish the fight I started. My burdens have at last become too much for me to bear alone, and that means they have fallen to you, Vic. All those years ago, I never dreamed it might one day come to this."

I looked at him. "Kronin, I can't carry your burdens. I've already failed. Delano has the sword now." A lump stuck in my throat although I tried to push it back. "There's nothing more I can do."

The God-King puffed out a lungful of smoke in perfect rings. He watched them float away before he turned back to me and grinned. He struck me as awfully serene for a guy who was steps away from dying.

"Why does it matter so much that Delano has the *Gladius Solis?*" Kronin asked.

I arched my eyebrows. "Uh...because that's the sword you forged from the magic stone. I listened to that whole thing, man. You can't pull some trick question crap on me."

His grin widened. "Sure, but who said the *Gladius Solis* was the only one of its kind?"

For about the third time that morning, my jaw practically hit the floor. "Say what now?"

Kronin inhaled. "It's exactly as I said. The *Gladius Solis* is currently unique—but it doesn't have to be." He flicked his gaze over to the centurion. "Would you bring me something to eat, old friend? I'm afraid my endurance is not what it used to be."

Marcus snapped to full attention. "Of course, my lord. Right away." He disappeared down a path toward the palace and Kronin directed me a similar way. We walked side by side and both of us limped slightly.

"What's this new weapon?" I asked him, curious.

"That's up to you, Vic," Kronin replied. "You're the one who will bring it to life."

The building we entered was separate from the palace and huge in its own right, towering high into the sky. The

God-King led me into the basement and along a mess of labyrinthian corridors to the door of a massive underground vault. It stood open enough for a person to slip inside, which was what we did. Torches lit up on the interior walls to banish the darkness.

I looked around. The vault was almost empty. A small pile of strange, glimmering rock lay near the middle of the floor. He went over, picked up the tiniest piece in his hand, and beckoned me closer. "Long ago, this Solis Stone was plentiful in Carcerum," he said. "This is all that remains."

I gazed at the metal. "There isn't that much," I remarked. "That's messed up. I thought you said the *Gladius Solis* was unique."

"It is." Kronin turned the small shard of stone in his palm. "There is more than one use for Solis Stone. How do you think gods are made?" He tapped his finger against it. "The creators shaped the gods from the stone and it granted them their powers. But they would be easy prey to a Solis weapon."

"That's why the sword works so well on them!" I exclaimed. "Holy crap! What are we waiting for? We have to make another one."

The God-King stopped me. "I want to tell you something first." His voice and eyes were somber. "No doubt you have noticed that Marcus, despite having been irrefutably killed some time ago, is able to regain his physical form and walk around here." He gestured to the medallion around my neck. "This pendant is infused with traces of Solis Stone which gives it the ability to preserve and restore spirits."

"Okay." I frowned. "I get it. There's more than one use. I

still want to make another sword."

He pressed on. "I can give you a choice. You can forge a new weapon, as you think you want to do. You can take this weapon back to the temple and use it to fight Delano. I must let you know that I have no knowledge of what that outcome will be." He glanced at the Solis Stone. "Or, you can choose to spend your days here in peace. With Marcus…and your family."

At first, I didn't think I heard him correctly. "Sorry?" I asked. "My family's gone."

Kronin gave me the look of a teacher who had to spend extra time with a particularly slow student. "As I said, Solis Stone preserves spirits. Here." He took my hand and placed my palm on the smooth, cold slab. "Keep your hand there," he said. "Speak their names."

He moved past me to wait outside the vault.

My heart did a weird little flutter. I could hear my pulse in my ears. My mouth went suddenly dry, and it was hard to conjure the voice I needed to say the right things. It seemed impossible to say their names, so I simply called them as I always had.

"Mom," I said. "Dad."

The surrounding stillness deepened. Murky shadows moved across the surface of the stone. One moment, I was alone in the vault, and the next, my parents were there in front of me.

"Victoria," my mother said quietly. "My goodness, how long it's been?" Her eyes, the same as mine, glittered with barely repressed tears.

My father smiled, his arm around her shoulders. "Still my little girl," he said.

## CHAPTER TWENTY-FIVE

The room was as dark as I could make it and the drapes that hung down over the bed were pulled tight, but I still couldn't keep my eyes closed. I lay on my back, looked at the canopy above me, and mulled over everything Kronin had shown me that day. The incredible beauty of his empty kingdom. The truth of his own history. My parents summoned to life years after their murders. I had finally made peace with the part of myself that had lusted after vengeance. I'd laid their ghosts to rest.

And yet, they were with me, no different than they had been the last time I saw them alive. It was like no time had passed at all, except that we all knew it had. I was so relieved to see they were happy and at peace. But I was also mortified. My mother and father were not violent people. I'd never imagined a scenario where they knew what happened to me after they died, much less one where we had to talk about it.

It was weird until my dad said he was proud of me. Then, it was awesome.

He'd given me one of his trademark bear hugs, the kind that lifted me off my feet. My mom had kissed my cheek and tucked a lock of hair behind my ear. So many things I never thought I'd be able to feel again, and I had them for those few moments. Part of me *did* want to hold on to them forever.

It was agonizing to take my hand off that stone and watch them fade away, a flash-grenade of grief in my chest. But that storm passed quickly, supplanted by the echoes of their love. Even now, I still smelled traces of my mother's favorite perfume.

I missed them so much. Seeing them again had made me painfully aware of the void they left behind. The notion that I could have that life again in Carcerum was sorely tempting. No pain, no war, no violence. Only me and my parents and Marcus, kicking back and eating all the weird, delicious fruit we wanted.

But no Deacon either. I curled up as he entered my mind and braced for the ruthless flood of emotions. The thought of leaving him with Delano filled me with guilt. Before I saw my parents, I had known I couldn't abandon him.

Did I still know that after?

"Ugh." I sat up in the bed. "Marcus?"

He didn't answer, so I closed my hand around the medallion and had a moment of panic when I found it cold. Then I remembered he wasn't in there.

"Oh, yeah." I shook my head, ran a hand through my hair, and swung my feet over the side of the mattress. Sleep would clearly not happen anytime soon. What I needed was a friendly ear.

Carcerum's sky was studded with diamond stars on a velvet backdrop. The moonlight bathed the land in a mythical silver glow, bright enough to light my way as I set out to find Marcus. I had no idea where his quarters were or if he even needed to sleep. I merely turned my brain off and tracked my inner compass. The old guy was basically a part of me by now anyway.

Still, it took a while to find him. Not that I minded exploring Carcerum at night. The whole place was like something out of a fairytale, one that always ended well. I wandered along the roads for about an hour while I kept a watchful eye out for any signs of a Roman centurion. At last, my gaze snagged on a light in the window of a smallish out-building. Its door was left slightly ajar. I went to the edge of the frame and peered inside.

Marcus stood in front of a large oval mirror. The glass was reflective, but not of anything in front of it. Shapes appeared to shift across its surface. I stepped into the building. "Hey, there you are."

Marcus glanced up. "Hail, Victoria," he said. "Sleep eludes you, I see."

I shrugged. "Nothing new there. What are you looking at?" I stepped beside him.

Marcus stared into the depths of the mirror. "It was once my job to watch Earth from here to make sure no Forgotten had broken Kronin's law. This mirror can show you anything in the world you desire to see, in the past and in the present. It has always helped to keep my vision clear."

In the silvery field of the glass, a slender man strode down a dark pathway. "What's on now?" I asked.

"We are witnessing the rise of our foe," Marcus said. A second later, the man turned to the side and I saw a glimpse of his face. It was Delano, younger and closer to the way he used to look. His hair wasn't too long yet, and his skin hadn't developed its sallow undertones, but I'd have known him a mile away. He had a mean ax in his hands.

We watched in grim silence as Delano brought that ax into a house and used it to hack through a whole family. He emerged bloody and superficially wounded by his own vicious enthusiasm but unmistakably triumphant.

"What the fuck?" I said. "Was that *his* family?" The legend Marcus had told me about Delano's sacrifice to Lorcan ran through my head. "All that crazy stuff people said about him was real."

"Yes," Marcus said. The image shifted to show Delano walking down another path as he wound his way toward a vaguely familiar temple. He was met by Lorcan. His hands were still covered in blood.

Then, Lorcan gave Delano a knife, which the man promptly used on himself. "Gross!" I exclaimed once it became apparent that the lump of flesh he held out to Lorcan was his own heart. He collapsed and died at his master's feet.

"This is so fucked," I said. The image shifted once more, and I couldn't look away.

Delano in the present filled the mirror. He was clearly inside his own temple, and his face was twisted into the most awful smile. The view switched suddenly.

I bristled. "Oh, fuck!" He had my crew strung up on the walls of his grand hall, primed for torture. I watched helplessly as he carved intricate designs into Maya's stomach with his own claws. Sweat poured down her face but the vet didn't make a sound.

"I know you know where the little rat is hiding," Delano said cheerfully. "And frankly, I'm running out of patience." He turned from Maya, lunged at Steph, and grabbed her by the throat. She gasped for air.

I heard Frank shout. "Get off her! I'll fucking kill you."

Delano laughed. "Oh, I doubt that very much." He bore down on Steph until her face began to turn blue and he let go to sneer as she choked for air. Relentless, he walked around to every one of my crew. Jules and Brax were close together and held hands. Delano pressed a red-hot chain link to her skin. She screamed but she did not break. Brax looked like he wanted to crack the planet in half.

The only one I couldn't see or hear was Deacon. My heart wanted to believe that was because he'd somehow managed to escape, but I knew better than to count on it. I desperately needed to know where he was. At the same time, I feared the answer so I kept my questions inside. To voice them would make it all too real.

In the glass, Delano threw his head back, an expression of sheer glee plastered over his face. He had never, ever looked happier. It made me want to puke.

And it made me absolutely furious. To stand at the window, so to speak, unable to take any sort of action, was torture in its own right. I barely noticed that my fingernails had drawn crescents of blood from my palms. I was too fixated on Delano and how far out of my reach he was.

"I take back everything I said about Carcerum being a paradise," I said. "I get it now. I fucking get it." There was nothing hidden from me—nothing in the whole damn world—but I couldn't influence any of it. So what did it matter?

Delano's face loomed large in the glass. He was mocking me. "Fuck!" I shouted. I swung before I thought. The mirror shattered and splinters skidded across the floor. I stood there glowering at its empty stand.

"Victoria?" Marcus asked.

I turned to face him. "I know what I have to do."

# CHAPTER TWENTY-SIX

Marcus opened his mouth, presumably to ask me what the hell I was talking about. I brushed past him before he could speak, eager to get back to the vault and put my plan in motion. He called after me from the door. "Victoria!"

"I'll meet you there!" I called back. "Trust me, Marcus. This can't wait!"

"I understand your urgency, but—" He caught up with me and pointed in a different direction. "If you plan to return to the vault, the building is that way."

"Oh." I changed course. "Right, I knew that."

He patted my back. "Worry not, my friend. I shall pretend I witnessed nothing."

To my surprise, the door to the basement vault room was open and a soft light emanated from inside. Marcus and I exchanged a glance as we descended the stairwell into the subterranean level. There was only one person it could really be. Sure enough, Kronin emerged from the vault in front of us with the last block of Solis Stone held in his arms.

Marcus stepped forward. "My liege," he said. "Let me help you."

The God-King shook his head. "Not this time, Marcus. The forging of a new Solis weapon is my duty and my honor." He looked at me. "Wait here inside the vault. I'll fetch you once the forge is primed." He hurried past me, his stride long and purposeful. We stepped into the vault's now empty belly.

"A new weapon?" Marcus asked.

"Yeah." I rubbed at the traces of dust on the floor with my toe. "Another sword is the only thing that'll defeat Delano, so we have to make one. Then we take it back to his stupid, ugly temple and we ruin his day with it. You're in, right?"

The centurion smiled. "Must you ask? Of course I will accompany you." He paused. "But not a sword."

I gave him a look. "It has to be a sword, Marcus. I won't go into that fight armed with a holy golf club."

"You do not understand," he said patiently. "The sword is an instrument of equality—swordsmen begin and end on equal footing, no matter the outcome. You have used it thus far to put down hordes of lesser beings, and it has certainly served you well, but it is not for slaying demons. For that, you require a spear."

"That's a load of crap," I said. "There are a million fairy-tales about knights who bring swords into dragon lairs. If it's good enough for Saint George, it's good enough for me." The deep whooshing sound of a kindled flame rushed to my ears and I glanced up to see a flood of warm light spread over the outside corridor. The burning hum of Kronin's forge resonated in the walls like a voice. Goosebumps stood up on my arms.

Marcus watched me knowingly. "Those fairytales were no doubt written by fat old men, not by experienced warriors such as yours truly." For emphasis, he dusted his shoulder plate with a dramatic gesture.

I rolled my eyes but laughed anyway. How amazing it was to be there in Carcerum with Marcus. A small miracle amid all the darkness of the last few weeks. "I'd bet my life that you've never written a shopping list, let alone an entire classic fairytale," I said.

"Well, I've lived my fair share," Marcus answered. "And I know the villain never dies in glory."

"No," I interjected. "That's the hero's job."

Marcus put his hands on my arms and stared deep into my eyes. A spark of intensity burned within him and charged his words. "Victoria, listen. You saw as well as I that Delano is a monster, that he always has been. Nothing in the universe or beyond could elevate him to the level of your equal. I must urge you not to create another sword, only to sully its edge with his blood. He is not even worthy to speak your name." Marcus took a deep breath. "Delano is but a worm. He deserves to die like one."

I grinned. "I knew there was a reason I missed you, old man. No one gives an inspirational speech like you do."

He puffed his chest out. "It is a talent I acquired in Rome. My efforts to pass it on to you have had middling results."

"Hey!" I prodded him lightly in the chest. "I'm very

inspiring if I do say so myself. Lord knows no one else gives speeches in the mess hall at Fort Victory."

"Your inspiration lies more in your actions than your words," Marcus said. "You have stepped up and carved your mark upon the face of humanity. They will remember you, alive or dead, for generations to come."

I raised my eyebrows. "At least if I die, it'll be as glorious as hell. I think I want a Viking funeral. Like with the boat and the fire. Burn me with all my shit, too, so nobody else can have it."

Marcus chuckled. "Again, you are mistaken," he said. "Heroes die in tragedies. And that is not the kind of tale we will write."

"Oh, so that makes this a comedy and I'm headed for a wedding instead? Thanks for—" I stopped talking as the sentimental side of my brain immediately thought about Deacon. I looked away abruptly. Sudden impatience overtook my heart, and I eyed the corridor in anticipation of Kronin's interruption. The forge's fire had built to a dull roar.

"It is almost time," Marcus declared. "I am so very proud of you."

"I couldn't have done it without you, buddy," I said. We were quiet for a few seconds, each of us deep in thought. "I wonder if he waited here because he knew what I'd do without him having to ask."

"Kronin is wiser than most," the centurion said and shifted his weight. "But perhaps it is foolish to call him wise above all else. He has overlooked true intentions in the past, has he not? I have no doubt he wanted to be sure this time."

"Why even give me the choice?" I mused, half to myself. Then I realized that seeing my parents had only hardened my resolve to stop Delano once and for all. I missed them, yes, but that wound had long ago begun its healing process. Even if they weren't with me, I could hold them in my heart until I met them again.

I couldn't build humanity from the unrecognizable mess Delano wished to create. There'd be nothing left, for one thing. We were a plague of insects that he sought to exterminate. He thought we were worthless.

I knew better than that.

A flickering shadow fell across the floor in the hallway and approached the threshold of the vault. Marcus and I both looked at Kronin who stood in the open doorway. The king's brilliant eyes locked onto mine. "Are you ready, Vic?" he asked.

I moved toward him. "There's no doubt in my mind."

"Excellent." Kronin nodded approvingly. "Your sword awaits."

"Not a sword," I responded and glanced over my shoulder at Marcus. "A spear."

## CHAPTER TWENTY-SEVEN

The forge was massive with a blazing inferno like a small star burning at its heart. The dry heat crackled on my skin and I squinted into the light. The Solis Stone sat atop the smithy in the center. Its surface had already begun to glow. The fire seemed to arc through the stone itself and infused it with its wild power.

"Take this," Kronin said and handed me a long-handled hammer. He had to raise his voice to be heard above the forge. The tool was astonishingly heavy. If I hadn't braced myself at the last second, I might have dropped it, but I tightened my grip and gave it a truncated test swing.

The weighted head dropped in a brutal downward arc.

"Good," said the god. "That's the kind of power we'll need." He walked to the smithy and motioned for me to move into position beside him. "I will hold the Solis Stone in place. You strike it and don't hold back." I looked at his bare hands and back at him. His beatific face held no trace of humor. "Trust me, Vic. I am the only one who has the strength. I can endure."

The breath I took filled my lungs with hot, dusty air. I squared my stance at the edge of the smithy, fixed my gaze on the raw, unshaped material, and raised the forge hammer. The flat side struck the Solis Stone with a shower of white-hot sparks, and at the same time, an agonized scream sliced through the chamber. I tensed, the hammer raised, and scanned the vicinity for the source of the sound.

Kronin leaned over the smithy. His hands anchored the far end of the stone and its power leaked through his skin. The muscles of his strong jaw clenched so tightly that they trembled. Sweat rolled down his brow. The veins in his neck and arms bulged. But when he spoke, he was resolute. I had never heard a steadier voice.

"I can endure," he repeated. "Do not stop. The fate of the world depends on this success. Push me from your thoughts and focus only on the task at hand. Go!"

The hammer rose and fell again and again. Each time, a geyser of sparks was followed by a tortured cry. I steeled my will until his suffering fused with the roar of the forge and layered itself into the ambient soundtrack of my work. After that, I didn't stop except to keep the perspiration from dripping down into my eyes. My strikes grew faster and more precise. The spear began to emerge beneath the heavy rain of blows.

Kronin's voice turned hoarse. I didn't allow myself to look at him, afraid I'd lose my nerve if I was disturbed by what I saw. I simply held the hammer tighter and leaned into the heat. My shirt clung to my back. Locks of hair streaked down the sides of my face and plastered onto my cheeks. The feeling in my arms slowly numbed. Still, I kept at it. When it was time to stop, Kronin would tell me.

And he did, in a sense. I followed through into my next strike when I noticed he no longer hung over the side of the smithy and struggled through the spear's creation. He lay crumpled on the floor, utterly spent with his eyes half closed. If I had considered him pale before, he was ghostly now.

"Take it up," he murmured. His voice, although frail, somehow still managed to carry to my ears. "Plunge it into the water and gaze upon your handiwork."

I did as I was told and tossed the spear into its first cold bath. Steam billowed from the water and obscured everything in a thick cloud. When I put my hand back in, the water was almost hot and my fingers closed around something that felt like a real weapon. The glistening spear emerged from the fog and still shed droplets that hissed into vapor on contact with the surface of the smithy. I held it as though it was made of glass and not an ethereal resource of the gods. Fine details that I hadn't carved slowly and subtly adorned the shaft. It reminded me, unsurprisingly, of the *Gladius Solis*.

I spun to feel the weight of the spear in my hands. The blade was light, nimble, and devastatingly sharp. I fumbled a little with the much longer shaft. "This will take some getting used to," I said, but I brimmed with the kind of pride that only comes with accomplishment. As much as I loved that fiery sword and as well as I'd learned to wield it, Kronin's original blade was a hand-me-down, an inheritance from Marcus. This spear was as much mine as it could possibly be. I examined it with a grin.

When I turned to show Kronin, my pride turned to concern in an instant. He lay where he had fallen beside the forge, motionless except for the uneven rise and fall of his chest. I set the spear down and ran to him. Behind me, footsteps entered the area.

"My liege!" Marcus exclaimed. "What happened?" We fell to our knees alongside the king.

Kronin smiled at us. "Thank you," he said haltingly. "For carrying me to the end of my long and winding path. Forging the final weapon required the last of my strength. I am afraid that very soon, I must leave you. For good, this time." Pure exhaustion seemed to erode his features. The ends of his words dropped off and I could sense him beginning to slip away.

"I'm sorry, Kronin," I told him. "This isn't the end you deserve."

The God-King chuckled weakly. "It's funny you should say that," he whispered. "Take care of this place in my absence and take care of humanity."

"I have to save it first," I told him.

He closed his eyes. "You will." His voice faded rapidly. "Regret nothing. I have never been prouder." One last breath rattled into his lungs and was expelled after a long lull. It carried his spirit away and left us kneeling over his body.

When I started to rise, Marcus stopped me. I was about to ask him why when the king's body changed and seemed to accelerate through millennia of aging in a matter of seconds. At the end, all that was left of Kronin, king of the gods, was a pile of dust.

I'd seen the process take place once before when

Marcus died in the slaughterhouse. The centurion sat for a moment longer and contemplated the ashes that had been his beloved sovereign less than a minute before. "It was true," he said quietly. "Kronin was human, and yet he was the one who managed to wrangle order out of this mess of chaos."

I pushed to my feet. The ever-present wound in my leg released a twinge of pain whenever I put weight on it. I bent and picked up the spear. "He's a tough act to follow," I told Marcus. "But someone has to do it."

The old Roman's solemn air of mourning morphed into peace as he joined me. We took one last shared look at the looming forge before Marcus doused its fire and rendered the beast dormant. He glanced at me, then at the spear in my hand. "It is time to return to Earth," he said. "Our work here—and Kronin's—is done."

I nodded. Neither of us made a move to disturb the remains of Carcerum's late ruler. He had earned eternal serenity at last and sleep in the shadow of the forge that birthed his legacy.

"Let's go." I lifted the spear clear of the floor and headed for the basement stairs. "I don't know how much time we have left."

## CHAPTER TWENTY-EIGHT

With Kronin dead, the true emptiness of Carcerum descended on the palace like a heavy black pall. As we crossed the throne room and banquet hall, it felt as if we waded along the ocean floor. The throne itself stood conspicuously vacant in the vast chamber. Part of me hoped it would never be occupied again.

"I was wrong before," Marcus conceded while he kept pace beside me. "This part of the story is a tragedy."

"It's not over yet," I replied. "We still have a whole lot of Forgotten ass to kick."

"For Kronin," the centurion declared.

"For mankind," I added.

The huge portal that led out of the realm set deep into the palace wall towered above us. It looked far too heavy to open on my own, but as we drew closer, my spear began to glow. The light intensified until it was impossible to look at it directly. I paused within arm's reach of the ancient door.

"Oh, shit." An unpleasant thought flitted through my brain. "You need to go back into the medallion, don't you?"

"Yes," Marcus said. "Unfortunately, the ending of my tenure on Earth destroyed my ability to inhabit it in a corporeal form."

"That blows," I said. "I'm really sorry. I wish there was something we could do."

"It matters not," he assured me. "If it means that I may remain by your side, I shall gladly make every sacrifice." He put a hand into his pocket and withdrew a closed fist. "Briefly, before we depart—I have brought you a modest gift." He opened his fingers and there, nestled in his palm, was a piece of the mirror I had shattered in anger. "It used to be much nicer. And larger. But earlier tonight, someone came in and broke it. I have absolutely no idea who that might have been."

I chuckled. "Sorry. I guess I'm much like a bull in a china shop sometimes." The mirror shard glinted but it remained blank. I slipped it into the lining of my coat for safekeeping before I turned my attention to the spear. Its current form simply wasn't practical at all. Walking with the thing held clear of the ground was awkward at best and horribly annoying at worst. I shifted my weight off my bad leg while I considered my options. Suddenly, inspiration struck like a bolt from the blue.

The spear's glow intensified again, and this time, the great door out of Carcerum swung open far enough to allow me through. I focused my will on the weapon like a laser, and it transformed into a harmless walking stick in my hand. My whole leg flooded with relief once I redistributed my weight.

"That's better," I said with a sigh of satisfaction. A constant blast of cold air rocketed into my face from the other side of the door. I stepped through, and my foot sank instantly into a few inches of fresh snow. A howling, snowy wind raked its fingers through my hair and the breath seemed to freeze in my lungs once again.

"It's good to be back," I gasped. Marcus's medallion regained its distinctive warmth and his voice sounded in my ears.

*It will be better to be back at sea level.*

I pulled the collar of my jacket up and tucked my chin down against the cold. "Agreed."

The wind kicked up flurries of snow and ice every second, which reduced visibility to almost nothing. I had, evidently, chosen to make my exit from Carcerum in the middle of an Earth-based storm atop the Himalayan peak that served as the connection between realms. The safest thing to do was to perhaps duck as low as possible and try to feel my way backward until I hopefully determined where I was. I'd barely begun the uncomfortable exercise that way when a voice cut through the gale.

"Vic? Is that you?"

I whipped my head around and searched for Shiva in the whiteout. My maternal instinct reared its rare and frustrated head. What the hell was that crazy kid doing on a mountaintop in the middle of a storm? Never mind that I was there too, or that he had likely come to find me.

"Shiva!" I called and hoped his name would carry far enough to be heard. "Where are you?"

"Vic?" he called again. I swung gingerly to peer into the whirling snow on the west edge of the summit. Shiva trudged into sight, hunched against the elements. My heart skipped a beat.

I waved like crazy until I was sure he'd seen me through the squall. The moment he moved within earshot, I said, "You should be at home, Shiva. You probably know that better than I do."

He shrugged. "I need help. We need help—the whole town. We need someone strong enough to kill gods." His big brown eyes peered at me from between layers of scarf. "You are the only one I could think of."

Distracted, I frowned at him. "Gods?" The last I'd seen, there hadn't been any in Shiva's town except the bizarrely peaceable Forgotten. "This is new."

He nodded. "It is. Just before sunset on the day you left, a god arrived. The entire town is held hostage. I am not sure what will happen to them." An edge of real fear underpinned his calm voice. "We must destroy this being by any means necessary. Please."

I ran my thumb along the warm wood of the walking stick where the edge of my spear would be. "Relax," I told him. "Keep your head on straight and show me the way. I'll take care of this."

Shiva turned on a dime like a damn mountain goat, and I swore he bounded down the sheer mountain face. It took so much effort to keep up that I didn't have the breath to call for him to slow the hell down a little. Soon, I resorted to a more or less blind slide down the route I thought he took and relied on the stick more and more in the low visibility.

*I have to say, the one thing I do appreciate about this noncorporeal arrangement is not having to do any of the physical work.*

"Ha ha," I muttered. "I think you missed your calling as a stand-up comedian."

I felt Marcus frown. *What other type of humorist is there?* He paused as if in thought. *I suppose he could be disabled, such that he would be unable to stand.*

"Ugh, Forget it." I levered myself away from a frozen boulder that protruded from the mountain. "Man, that kid is like lightning. I hope he waits for us when he gets down there."

I soon saw that my prayers had been answered as I identified Shiva's bluish silhouette near the bottom of the mountain. He beckoned frantically to me. There was no rickshaw to carry us into town, but my pace was probably faster anyway, even with the limp.

"Do not let her see you," Shiva implored. "She is suspicious of everyone and will gladly fight."

I shrugged. "I might be interested in that, depending on the circumstances." Shiva showed real concern at that. I clapped him on the shoulder with the hand that didn't hold my disguised spear. "Don't sweat it, kid. By now, I'm as close to a professional as you'll find."

And frankly, I was a little excited by the prospect of getting back to business. Delano had proven that he was nothing to fuck with. Whoever had rolled into Shiva's hometown was about to serve as the perfect warmup to get me back in the game.

## CHAPTER TWENTY-NINE

A quarter of a mile outside of town, where the road began to widen into the main stone-paved street of Shiva's home, the kid motioned for me to use stealth rather than speed. Our pace slowed significantly as we concentrated on the need to be as quiet as possible. He seemed to think the element of surprise was crucial to our well-being. With my spear in hand, I wasn't so sure it would matter. The fighter in me cracked her knuckles and literally itched for a fight. I'd had my rest and it was time to get back in the mix.

The angular, stacked houses gradually took shape through the storm and the central street rolled out before us. This time, our surroundings were empty. Doors and windows hung open and fires smoldered unattended on open hearths. I snuck a glance inside one or two of the homes on our way past. There were signs of life everywhere, but it was as if the people had simply dropped everything and walked away.

"Where are they?" I asked Shiva, my voice barely audible. He pointed up the street toward the center of the town. A weird, dense mass blocked my view past a certain point. It soon became apparent that this was a mob that consisted of the entire town. They'd been herded into the open space in the road and now stood unmoving, facing forward. No one spoke, and their silence was eerily ominous.

The scene struck me as disturbingly familiar. I'd seen the same blank, passive stares over and over again in places where a god tried to exercise their authority. Rocca's minions, Oxylem's lumber camps, and the Midwest town overrun by ogres. They always wanted the same thing from humanity—total compliance. And unfortunately, they were all in a position to enforce that demand.

Shiva pulled me into one of the alleys between the houses and peered around the corner into the roadway. "She has trapped the entire town," he told me. "I was lucky to escape without notice."

*This god reeks of overconfidence,* Marcus told me. *Take her down swiftly.*

I nodded toward the front of the throng. "She's up there?"

The boy nodded, and I slipped out of the alley to join the masses. Those gathered there barely glanced at me as I began to work my way slowly forward. I kept my ears open for any clue as to who this unidentified god might be, and it didn't take long for a woman's harsh, grating voice to reach me through the clear, cold air.

"Rise!" she screeched. "Look at yourselves, stooping to the level of this filth. These mortals are unworthy of even an ounce of your blood. Follow me to glory, my brothers and sisters. Destroy the humans. Let them die with their forsaken world. Think of it as mercy, if you must consider them at all."

The humans kept their eyes downcast, but the Forgotten scattered throughout the crowd looked toward the voice. I weaved carefully in and out until I paused as close to the front as I dared. The god held court in the middle of the street and glared at her unwilling subjects. She was tall and curvy, a beautiful, cruel-faced woman from the waist up. Torrents of inky hair curled down her back. Ruby-red lips framed her needle-sharp teeth. Her lower half smoothed into a creepy, limbless body that glimmered with scales. The tip of her coiled tail twitched back and forth.

Suddenly, her eyes snapped to the onlookers in the front row and panned hungrily across their faces. She lunged forward, grabbed a small, bestial Forgotten by the scruff of its neck, and yanked it off the ground. Her muscular tail wrapped around its torso. The Forgotten's hooves attempted a few futile kicks but the tail's grip tightened around the creature's ribcage. The crack of breaking bones cut through the deep silence and several humans flinched.

"If you care about this little whelp, come and stop me," the god taunted. She stuck out her slimy tongue and waggled it obscenely. "I don't see any challengers. Cowards, all of you."

Another rib snapped beneath the crushing force of her tail. Her prey emitted a gasped squeal. Its eyes had begun to bulge in their sockets.

"How can you choose the scum of this earth over one of your own?" she demanded. Anger flashed white-hot in her eyes. "They are not fit to wash their own blood from your feet."

"Stand down, hag." The voice was deep and resonant and commanded attention. It came from an extraordinarily tall creature that resembled a hybrid of a werewolf and a tree giant. His skin was rough like bark, but each branch arm ended in sharp, striking claws. The eyes in his wise old face burned yellow and a mane of foliage flowed from his head. "Those of us who came here to seek refuge from your kind will not betray our mortal siblings. Begone, or we will drive you out, no matter what the cost."

The god flared her nostrils and hissed disdain. "Our kind?" Her indignation gave rise to a shrill guffaw of delight. "Do you honestly believe that this layer of human scum is your family? There are no words to describe how far beneath you they are. Answer the call of your superior blood. Accept the privilege that is your right and which your strength bestows upon you. Do not fritter your days away like this, doing nothing and idolizing a worthless peace." Her expression switched instantly to disgust. "You owe them nothing. They should surrender their lives in deference to a greater power."

The old Forgotten shook his head. A hand grabbed onto my wrist from behind, and when I turned, Shiva was there. "What do we do?"

I grinned at him. "We show this bitch what real power looks like."

With that, I stepped through the people who blocked my path and out of the captive audience. The town held its breath, human and Forgotten alike. Every eye was glued on me.

The god swiveled in my direction. Her initial confusion quickly gave way to insult and rage when she realized I was simply some jerk who'd showed up to dispute her authority. Her lips curled into a sneer at the edges. She released her grip on the small, miserable Forgotten, who dropped to the ground with a heavy thump.

"You must be joking." The god laughed. "I'm almost offended that this is the best you have to offer. There is nothing an ignorant, crippled girl can do to stop me."

I tightened my hand around the top of the walking stick. The haft of the spear hummed within its magical disguise. "You forgot one very important detail," I told her. "I'm ignorant, crippled, and armed to the fucking teeth." In an instant, the stick was a spear and I hurled its shining point directly at the god's ugly heart. Her body offered no resistance. She uttered an ear-piercing screech as she fell to the freezing stone, mortally wounded but not quite dead. Thick, violet blood pumped from her new wound.

The townspeople gasped collectively and shoved up behind me for a better look at the downed god. She tried in vain to right herself in the spreading pool of blood. It seeped into the ground and trickled along the cracks in the street.

I held up my hand to summon the spear and it flew back into my palm. "Whose blood from whose feet?" I asked before I turned my back on her to face the mixed population of the mountain town. Human faces regarded me calmly alongside Forgotten with no traces of fear or apprehension. I nodded. This *was* the way it could be. The way it should be for the future.

"This is a town that has thrived in the midst of a

horrendous war," I declared. My voice seemed amplified and strong. Shiva began a running translation into the native tongue. The eyes on me were rapt with interest. "You have thrown off the shackles of prejudice and intolerance, and in doing so, created a haven where all manner of life can feel safe. The heart of your town beats strongest as you live as neighbors and work together in harmony."

A murmur of agreement rippled through them. People began to smile, tentatively at first but with growing confidence.

"That's right," I told them. "And now, I encourage you to keep that cooperative spirit alive by sending this foolish entity to her grave." At my back, the god no longer thrashed with such desperate ferocity. She lay on her side and wheezed and gurgled. Her distress was drowned out by the cheer that went up after Shiva translated my last sentence. I smiled. "Have at it."

The crowd surged forward and released bloodthirsty, rallying cries up to the heavens. I moved against the living current and walked away. Presently, another cry joined the cacophony produced by the town. The god screamed as they fell on her and presumably tore her to pieces. The shriek pierced shrilly through the roar of the crowd for a few seconds and then it was gone.

*You are smiling, Victoria,* Marcus observed. *What makes you so happy?*

I made no effort to conceal my joy. For the first time since we'd arrived in Indiana, a sense of inner peace had taken root in my heart. "Because, Marcus..." I clasped the medallion warmly in my hand. "I know how I will defeat Delano."

# CHAPTER THIRTY

I sat behind the wheel of the new SUV and stared out the windshield at the stark expanse of Indiana cornfields. The sky stretched on forever over miles of dirt and snow, a landscape that had been so far away only days before. That morning, I had touched down at yet another teeny regional airfield a hundred miles east in another miniscule plane. The journey, at least, had been calmer and less death-defying. It had included a boat this time, too, and a short ride on a commuter train somewhere in Asia that was empty except for the operator and me. A slideshow of devastation had flashed by the windows while we raced through tunnel after tunnel. Even the underground stations were trashed.

After the train, I proceeded through a never-ending series of cars and trucks. I had hoped that Asia might have fared better than the West during the gods' takeover, but the snapshot of the continent that I witnessed told a very similar story. My travels didn't take me through the heart of any major metropolises, but I had to assume the destruction there was comparable to New York—or worse. With so many people so close together, they wouldn't stand a chance

By the time I finally rolled out toward Indiana, I had seen enough variations of empty countryside to last me a dozen lifetimes. Of course, the last two hours had been nothing but the American flavor of farmland. All the over-grown grass and dreary winter palette had begun to blend together after the vibrant colors of Carcerum.

I still struggled to believe that I'd actually been there, stood at the base of Kronin's throne, walked the footpaths around his palace grounds, and knelt beside the forge where he died. It could have been yesterday, or it could have been millennia before.

Still, all I had to do to prove those memories real beyond a shadow of a doubt was look to my right at the spear that lay across the passenger seat. Once I left the Himalayas behind, it never looked like a walking stick again. I liked to feel its true shape as a reminder of where I had come from—and what I had to do.

I wondered if Delano knew his days were numbered. If he didn't already, he soon would.

The SUV bumped over the uneven, scarred ground and headed due west toward the temple. I knew exactly which landmark I searched for, and eventually, I saw it —a lone truck that stood as the last remnant of our first ill-fated mission. To see it there where I had abandoned it in my mad dash to South Asia brought a rush of every emotion I had experienced over the last week. Anger that things had gone so poorly. Fear that I was too late to save my friends. Sadness that we'd cut it so damn close that this was what the situation had come to.

I pulled to a stop alongside the vehicle, snatched up my spear, and drew it across my lap. There was no need to step out into the cold Midwestern morning just yet. I'd come there to wait again, after all. This time, however, I knew my contacts would show.

I released a deep sigh and cranked the seat lever so I could stretch out flat on my back. "It's bad out there," I said to Marcus. "Maybe worse than I thought it would be, which seems as stupid as hell, given what we know."

*We are certainly not at an advantage,* he agreed. *It is difficult to accurately gauge god activity in a period of time as short as we spent near the mountains, but it is safe to deduce that the effect has been more or less similar to what is happening here.* He paused. *We must hope against all other hopes that slaying Delano will be enough to begin to rectify the damage he has done.*

"Okay, yes," I said. "That's all true. But there's a silver lining." I stretched my tired, achy limbs while I talked and willed energy back into them. "It's clear that god activity is significantly diminished. We've hardly seen anything so far, not even big groups of Forgotten."

*Indeed,* Marcus replied and once again, I could easily sense his frown. *You deserved the respite, but I do find it somewhat worrying. This journey has never been tranquil.* Again, he paused and I imagined his face as he searched for the right words. *It strikes me as a bad omen.*

I tried to cheer him up. "Lighten up, Doom and Gloom," I said. "Even if you're right, there's not much we can do about it now. We made it back here. We can't turn around. The only way to go is directly ahead."

*Out of the frying pan, into the fire,* he said.

I grinned. "Hey, there you go."

The conversation ebbed into companionable silence. I slipped my hand into my coat and withdrew the shard of magic mirror Marcus had given me as we left Carcerum. It still didn't reveal much that I could understand. If I stared into the silvered glass, images took form, but I had no way to control who or what I saw and no frame of reference for the window in history. Ten seconds ago and ten years ago were exactly the same, as far as I could tell.

I put the mirror piece away and leaned my head back again to stare at the underside of the SUV roof. The calm before the storm weighed heavily on me. I grew fidgety when I thought about all the things that could go wrong or might have already gone wrong. As always, I cracked my knuckles and tapped my toes inside my boots. Suddenly, it was impossible to sit still.

Irritated by my own impatience, I sat up, opened the door, and hung my legs out sideways. The first slap of cold air momentarily chased my thoughts away, but they crashed back the second I acclimated to the temperature change. With the spear held firmly across my legs, I traced its sturdy shape—simpler than the *Gladius Solis,* but not bad for someone who didn't know shit about forging. Of course, that probably had more to do with the weird magic of the god realm, but I let myself take some credit. I needed the confidence boost to fight my nerves.

*Worry not, Victoria,* Marcus said. *You can do this. You have trained for it. And you are the last hope for the future.*

I snorted. "No pressure. Oh, well. At least I have the spear."

"You have us too, Vic." The gruff, gravelly voice came from the far side of the pickup. I glanced through the window to see Smitty, Amber, and a thirty-person crew smiling into the cab. The old blacksmith snapped a salute. "Were contingent, reporting for duty."

I scrambled out of the vehicle and ran to hug him and his granddaughter. "Oh, hell yeah! You actually made it."

Amber gave me an unimpressed look. "Of course we made it, Vic. We're freaking professionals." She squeezed me tightly around the middle. "Besides, we wouldn't miss this for the world." Her brows arched. "Nice spear, by the way. Did you get sick of the sword?"

"Uh, in a manner of speaking." I glanced at the forces they'd brought from the Pacific Northwest. "How'd you cart this many people long distance?"

Smitty cleared his throat. "Well…" He shoved his hands in his pockets. "We'll just say it was a chore. Did you ever try to put thirty werewolves through a security line?" He arched his woolly eyebrows and chuckled. "Ah, but it doesn't matter. We're here, and you're here, and we have a large bone to pick, don't we?"

"Yeah," I said grimly. "Yeah, we sure fucking do."

# CHAPTER THIRTY-ONE

The scenery had been bad on my first mission, but it had gotten even worse since then. Great swaths of the frozen dirt, which had been reasonably packed a couple weeks before, were now churned into an icy slurry that made the journey surprisingly treacherous. Signs of an ongoing struggle were strewn everywhere, including large, dark splashes of what was probably blood.

"Something went down out here," Smitty commented. "Serious enough that it scared them all off, I guess." He made a full-circle turn and his single blue eye scoured the surroundings. "It was like this out west, as well. Too damn quiet. They ought to be crawling out the woodwork."

"It's boring!" Amber piped up. "Sniping is way more fun than doing chores in the base."

Her grandpa smirked. "She says that like I can even keep her inside for more than fifteen minutes at a time. Always patrolling, gathering information, and spying on whoever."

"It was real busy for a while after you left," Amber told

me. "Maybe for a week or something like that. I saw a whole parade of gods go through the forest. Really crazy stuff. One guy was basically a dragon—horns out to here, wings out to there, all that good stuff." She paused to sift through her memories. "We had some run-ins with a few of them, but they seemed to move fast and I don't think they wanted trouble. It looked like they were on their way somewhere." She frowned slightly. "Weird. I mean, where do they have to go? They can do whatever the hell they want, right?"

"One would think so," I agreed. "But I suspect that we may have missed the bigger picture here."

*I don't like it, Victoria,* Marcus said. *Something must be brewing beneath the surface. This is Delano we are dealing with.*

It was a statement I couldn't disagree with, even if I wanted to. Delano began as an Apprenti of Lorcan. It was only natural that he'd be obsessed with shadow, secrecy, and plans upon plans. His machinations definitely went several levels deep.

"That crazy jackass," I muttered. "What the hell does he think he's doing?" I had a bad feeling that we were about to find out in no uncertain terms.

We trudged onward and slipped and slid over the torn-up snow and soil. More blood had splattered over scorch marks and chaotic, churned-up tracks. A little before the one-mile line, the tremendous stillness was broken by a resonating crash.

Amber jumped. "What was that?" she demanded, her eyes wide. Another soon followed.

Smitty furrowed his brow. "It sounds like two mountains having a boxing match," he said. "Is that yelling I hear?"

A third reverberated over our heads and deep, thunderous voices bickered indistinctly back and forth.

I smiled. "You know, your guess isn't that far off, Smitty. And I think these might be a couple of mountains I know." I increased my pace and left my bewildered cohorts to follow as best they could. Up ahead, I located two enormous hulking shapes armed with tree-sized clubs who swung at each other in the vast open space. Each time the clubs connected, chunks of wooden shrapnel exploded everywhere. I ducked as a piece zinged past my ear.

"Whoa!" Amber yelled as she came up behind me. "Are they gonna kill each other?"

"Nah," I said and ducked again. "They're only horsing around." As they both readied themselves for two more mighty swings, I cupped my hands around my mouth and yelled, "Hey, guys! You're supposed to be back at Brax's barricade."

They immediately ceased their altercation and peered around for the source of my voice. When they finally noticed me and my group, big grins spread across their faces.

"Human lady," said the one on the right. He shouldered his club. "Good to see you. Am glad you safe." He hunkered carefully into a sitting position and rested his chin on his hands. The other did the same.

"Are you guys twins?" Amber asked.

They blinked their enormous mono-eyes at her. "Do we look same?" they asked. "We not even brothers."

"Oh," she said sheepishly. "I mean...yeah. Sorry."

The giants looked at one another and back at us before they burst into earth-shaking fits of laughter. Tremors rumbled under our feet as they kicked their heels on the ground. A small fissure opened not too far from where we stood and Amber gave me a worried glance.

"Twins!" roared the left giant. He coughed and sucked in a deep breath. "Funny tiny girl. No. He much uglier than me."

The right giant grunted and jabbed a massive thumb at his friend. "It okay. He the dumb one."

Lefty chuckled. "Yeah," he said.

I suppressed a smile. "Do you fine gentlemen know what in the hell is going on around here?" I asked. "I didn't think I'd see you this far in."

They exchanged a glance. "We guard wall," Righty said. "Like Brax say. We tell humans to go away. Not safe. Humans too small." For emphasis on this point, he touched me very gently on the crown of my head with his finger. "Get squished."

"And then what?" I prompted.

A cloud of confusion crossed Lefty's broad face. "Whole human herd came," he said. "Lots and lots of humans and not-humans. We try to stop, but no work. So, we follow." He nodded his massive head in the direction of the temple. "They want go there. But we don't. We stay out."

"That's the smartest thing you've ever done," I told them. "Tell me what you mean by 'not-humans.' Did you see animals in that herd?"

"No, no." Righty waved his giant mitt. "Not-humans like us. But smaller."

Lefty added, "Much smaller. We biggest."

"Like gods?" I continued to fish for something specific. Trying to get these guys to communicate was an exercise in patience and Twenty Questions. "Or something else?"

"Gods," Righty confirmed. "And not-gods."

"All right, so we have humans, not-humans, gods, and not-gods," I said. "How many were there?"

Lefty's eye opened wide. "A lot," he told me. "A lot-lot." He spread his arms as a general indicator of measurement. "Look like whole world."

*Yes,* Marcus murmured. *This is precisely what we did not want.*

I made a face. "Why would he—" Then it struck me like a ton of bricks. "Oh. Oh, shit. He's on the universe's biggest power trip."

"I don't know what you're talking about, but I'm glad you seem to understand what's going on," Amber said.

"It's…well, it's not that complicated." I sighed. "I lost the sword last time I was here. Delano's had it since then, and I guess it's made him think he's entitled to force the entire planet to bow at his feet."

Smitty scoffed. "So you think he's rounded them up to do just that?"

"Yeah." I shrugged. "The dude's a cocky prick. That's all there is to it. He wants to be above everyone else."

Amber drew her gun. "He's gonna be on the floor when I'm done. I'll kneecap him from a hundred yards out. He won't even have a chance to see it coming."

I grinned. "I like your moxie, Amber. But it won't even be that difficult. He was nice enough to solve one of our biggest problems for us."

"Aw." She holstered the weapon on her back again and

exaggerated a pout. "If I don't get to shoot any bad guys out here, I'm gonna be pissed."

"Don't worry," I said. "I'm sure you'll have a chance once we're inside. And I know exactly how we'll get there."

Amber's eyes lit up. "Ooh, yes! I *love* this kind of sneaky stuff!"

"I know." I motioned for everyone to draw in close. The giants tilted their heads to listen. "All right, team. The plan is simple. Listen closely, and don't fuck it up."

# CHAPTER THIRTY-TWO

Our crew adopted a more circuitous route as we pushed into the heart of Delano's territory. We needed to find one of those caravans the giants had mentioned and insinuate ourselves into it without arousing suspicion. From there, we could easily infiltrate the temple.

But timing was everything. Obviously, the Weres needed to wolf out, but if they did it too soon, we would simply ask to be caught wandering the fields. I took a couple recon scouts ahead of the main group so that we would have ample warning. When we finally crept up on the back end of a caravan, I sent the scouts back to tell the crew. Then, I tucked myself away somewhere within sight of the transport. The spear transitioned into a walking stick once more.

The large group moved painfully slowly because everyone was exhausted and dragged their feet. All the humans and most of the Forgotten had downcast eyes but a few Forgotten stared defiantly ahead. The atmosphere, in general, was utterly dismal.

I waited until I heard the crew fall into place around me. Each of my Weres was ready to go in full, hairy were-wolf regalia. I told them to look as run-down as possible, and to not make any sudden moves. Smitty's silver blade arm was smeared with mud to hide its meticulously polished luster.

"Go." I motioned toward the back of the caravan. "Now!"

We broke out of hiding and attached ourselves to the back of the caravan one or two at a time. As with all the other disheartened crowds I had seen, no one reacted to our appearance. We gradually eased forward through the ranks so that we could finally see the front. Word got back to me that the caravan leaders were buff-ass super-demons with giant leathery wings who apparently wielded pitchforks.

Amber's response to this information was, "Isn't that kind of cliche?"

"I guess so," I said. "But I suppose they are leading a mob to a place of worship."

She cast her gaze around. "I don't know if you can even call these guys a mob," she said. "No one's done anything rebellious despite having complete freedom of movement. No one's incited violence or even tried to run. I think they've all given up." A hint of sadness colored her words. "I've seen this before. Back when Oxylem was in charge and gathered people as slaves, they all looked exactly like this. Total zombies, doing whatever he asked."

"Well, if you ask me," I said. "I think it's time to put a smile on those faces."

Before I could actually do anything, a strange sensation in my chest caught my attention. I dropped back into the crowd among my friends and fished the piece of mirror from my inside coat pocket. The surface of the shard was warm to the touch, like Marcus's medallion whenever he talked to me.

I flipped it over to study the latest fleeting image and almost dropped it underfoot immediately. A wild rush of excitement surged through my body. Whatever Delano had done or planned to do, Deacon was still alive. A grin stretched my lips before the picture changed a little, and my entire heart crushed inward in agony. It was still Deacon in the mirror, but now, his face was twisted in horrible agony and his mouth opened in a scream I thankfully couldn't hear.

My chest constricted once more to see him like that. I wanted to puke and cry at the same time. The depth of his pain was conveyed so intensely that I knew beyond a shadow of a doubt that he was dying. Delano had him sealed away somewhere and slowly tortured him to death.

Did the monster know I had the mirror? I doubted it, but then again, I knew better than to put anything past him. His sadistic cruelty knew no bounds. Maybe he *did* know somehow and used the knowledge to try to wear me down or get me to break so I'd be easy prey. I told myself that meant it was possible that Deacon's torture was faked and that it was only an illusion to hurt me instead.

But I knew better. Delano would never fake torture if

he had the option to enjoy the real thing. Again, I wanted to puke. To remain in that massed caravan of despair seemed impossible now, but to blow our cover would have been a disaster.

I positioned and repositioned the mirror shard in a desperate attempt to identify where Deacon was. He was sweaty and pale. Blood was smeared on the side of his face and a cut on his lower lip oozed around the swelling. His body convulsed.

The last thing I saw was his eyes rolling back into his head before the glass went dark. I shook it and flicked the surface with my finger but with no response. The sour taste of panic filled the back of my throat. Deacon was literally dying, and I'd been worried about blowing our cover?

"Fuck that," I said out loud. I needed to find him as fast as humanly possible. I could almost hear his clock slowly wind down.

With my heart in my throat, I worked my way to the perimeter of the group, determined to slip away surreptitiously into the surrounding field. The problems with this course of action were that the fields provided almost no real cover during daylight hours and the perimeter of the caravan was under constant guard. One of the demons blocked me with his body and stared at me through piercing reddish eyes.

"Get back in line," he commanded. He held his pitchfork firmly in one solid fist. I thought briefly that I should simply use the spear. I was sure I could do it and the jackass would die instantly, but a move like that would compromise our entire mission. All hell would break loose.

"Back in line," the demon repeated and his eyes narrowed. "I will not ask again."

Reluctantly, I shuffled back into the crowd. The demon kept his eyes on me for a while and I sensed his stare. Man, I so wanted to kill him. I wanted to kill all of them and race ahead until I found Deacon. Seething rage boiled in the back of my brain and clouded rational thought with pure emotion.

Still, logic prevailed. I knew deep down that there was far too much at stake to risk anything monumentally stupid. I closed my eyes without slowing my pace and counted to ten in my head. My breathing settled and the red-hot rage cloud dissipated somewhat. "Hold on, Deacon," I whispered to no one in particular. "Hold on."

"Vic, what the heck are you doing?" Amber hissed. "Is something wrong? Do we need to call it off?"

"What? No." I shook my head vehemently. "No, no. Everything's fine."

She didn't look convinced but didn't pursue the subject and I made no effort at conversation. My head might have been moderately more rational, but it was still full of noise. I clenched and unclenched my fingers over the top of my walking stick. The throb in my leg suddenly felt stronger and more insistent. I fought a ridiculous urge to push out of my skin.

The caravan stopped and the demons in front yelled something to the guards on the sides. They all snapped to attention. Through a gap in their otherwise impenetrable wall, I saw the base of the mountain of rubble rear up before us. My gaze followed its line all the way to the top. From that vantage point, the temple itself was barely visible but I gazed fixedly at where I knew it would be. I knew Deacon was in there somewhere and there was no way in hell that I would leave that place without him.

## CHAPTER THIRTY-THREE

The march continued and didn't falter, even when the terrain turned craggy and rough. The winged guards goaded everyone forward and berated us constantly in a number of different languages. They cracked their barbed tails like whips at anyone who dared to resist or fell behind. One insubordinate Forgotten was unceremoniously heaved off the side about fifty feet up. No one else in his vicinity made any further protest.

I climbed along with the masses while I gritted my teeth and seethed on the inside over my inability to do anything other than wait for an opportunity. What I wanted to do was start a brawl and escape to look for Deacon in the confusion. Five years prior, I would probably have done it. Now, however, a little voice in the back of my head constantly reminded me of my duty.

His name was Marcus. *Bide your time, Victoria. Do not throw everything away for a moment of gratification. Deacon's salvation will mean nothing if you are both destroyed in the aftermath.*

The logical side of me knew that he was right and I struggled to take his words to heart. To punish countless others for a selfish motive in this scenario would be unforgivable. The odds were too desperate. I didn't even have an inkling of where Deacon might be, but I still had to wrestle that primal urge into submission. The nearest guard was so close and never so much as even glanced at me—the ultimate temptation that simply rubbed salt into my wounded heart.

I took a deep breath and held it until my lungs felt about to burst. The long exhale helped me drag my crazy nerves under control. I managed to force my hands to cease the endless clenching and unclenching around the head of my stick. The caravan wound its way through switchbacks and angled relentlessly upward toward the temple. Someone else fell with a shriek but we continued without even a slight pause.

Eventually, the sound of rushing water became more powerful than the desolate drummed footsteps of our forced march. We finally crested the edge of the mountaintop onto the temple's plateau. The boulder at the corner immediately drew my gaze, the god still chained to spill water down into the river below. Its eyes—pure white —were wide, frightened, and agonized.

Behind that boulder, thick metal bars rose ten feet or higher along the back perimeter of the plateau. They formed a holding pen secured by a guarded gate that yawned open as the demons shoved us through. The temple stood beyond our reach but not out of sight like a pompous, glowing frog. It was open, too. I could see the first of the twisted pillars that lined the central hall.

The crowd surged forward and bustled me roughly along. Amber grabbed my wrist to keep us from getting separated. We ended up crammed against the far side of the pen. My cheek pressed briefly against the bars, and I noticed something that made me pause and stare.

Off to the side, a host of gods waited. They all looked incredibly awkward like they were at a party full of guests they didn't know. Most constantly cast fearful glances in the direction of the boulder that weighed the water god down. They would've had to walk past it to reach the place where they stood.

I was sure Delano had done that deliberately. He was a big fan of sending messages. Now, I had one for him.

The ocean of bodies around Amber and me jostled relentlessly as more and more humans and Forgotten entered the pen. The air smelled like sweat, fur, fear, and who knew what else. The longer I stayed there and endured the constant push and thrust, the thinner my already worn patience stretched. Finally, I dragged my hands down over my face and groaned. I couldn't take it anymore. It was find Deacon or bust.

I nudged Amber. "Hey, get into position as best you can and wait for a signal," I told her. "It should be relatively easy in this mess. There's no way for them to keep an eye on you for long."

Amber nodded. "Okay. Although I have to say that I feel some hardcore déjà vu right now."

Her words barely registered as I eased through the cover provided by the massive group. The temple loomed to my right, but I needed a way out of the pen first. Near the farthest back corner, I encountered a small commotion. Security dragged some beefy, horned lunkhead away. One of his horns had broken off at the curve. I looked at him as he was carried past and then in the direction he'd come from. There was a noticeable chip in one of the metal bars, and one of them was bent—not significantly so but enough for me to squeeze through. The fit was tight and it put way too much pressure on the gash in my leg. I powered through the pain and slid out on the other side.

Only a few people had seen me and most of them instantly pretended not to. One woman glanced at the small gap as if she wanted to follow. After a moment's thought, she whipped around to face forward. I ducked away as a guard strolled past to make sure the disturbance had really been settled.

*Close call,* Marcus remarked. He sounded amused rather than scolding. *To the end, you live on the knife's edge.*

"You know what they say," I told him. "To thine own self be true."

He scoffed. *No one has said that for thousands of years.*

It felt really good to break out of that claustrophobic prison, but I was nervous to be out in the open. No cover existed on the plateau except for the boulder, and that was too far away to be a practical option. I was more or less completely exposed.

"Hey, lady!" Some of the captives still on the inside tried to get my attention. They pointed forward toward the corner I now approached and mouthed the word "guard." I froze and listened intently. Sure enough, heavy footsteps sounded on the adjoining side and moved steadily closer. The prisoners shuffled to make space, which I didn't understand at first. Then it occurred to me that they expected I would give up and try to return to the pen before I was discovered.

Instead, I gave them a thumbs-up and whispered, "Thank you!"

I ran to meet the guard head on and kept the spear hidden as long as I could until my gaze locked onto his big, ugly face. He was some kind of armored golem, bigger than the ones I'd seen in DC and far meaner. He grinned when he saw me.

Still in motion, I grinned back. He grabbed with one huge hand but I hopped nimbly out of his grasp, drew the spear back, and forced it between his teeth. The blood that gurgled out of his throat cut off any kind of death scream and he dropped like a sack of bricks. I plucked my spear out, vaulted over the body, and went on my way.

None of the prisoners made a sound. Their overwhelming passivity now worked in my favor. Still, I was happy when I could veer away from the side of the pen and angle toward the temple itself. From what I could see, it seemed like the front entrance was the only one and at first, my heart sank. Delano might not have posted anyone there on my first visit, but now that he was looking for me, he had to have increased the guard presence. I hesitated and my mind raced before an idea pushed into clarity. I glanced at the spear. "Man, I hope this works."

The wall of the temple was made of fancy, polished stone, but it was no match for a Solis weapon. The spear stuck solidly immediately below the slanted edge of the roof. I wasted a fraction of a second while I wondered if it would hold before I decided it didn't matter. I would do this anyway. With a deep breath, I held my hand up, palm out, and willed myself to join the spear rather than the other way around.

"Please work," I whispered and scrunched my eyes shut. "Please—" In an instant, my body dangled over open air and I instinctively closed my fingers around the shaft of the weapon in the nick of time. I braced my feet against the top of the wall, climbed onto the roof, crouched down, and pulled my spear free.

*Very good, Victoria!* Marcus said proudly. *Your innovation can be quite impressive.*

I frowned. "I must ask that you not give me a performance review while I try to save lives." One life, specifically. One very important life. "We'll talk about a promotion after this is over."

With the spear slung onto my back, I dropped prone and crept along the roof on my stomach while I kept the spread of the plateau in my periphery. Guards circled the pen like sharks, inside and outside. They continued to thrust prisoners in through the gate like livestock held for slaughter.

A domed skylight was positioned in the center of the temple roof. It was dark, however, and as I leaned close to peer through the glass, I realized that it was too high up for the light in the lower part of the hall to reach. The sheer vertical distance made me nervous, but I thought back to my plane ride and my stormy climb in the Himalayas. Delano's temple was nothing compared to that.

With the edge of the spear, I cut a hole carefully in the curved glass large enough for me to fit through and managed to prevent the loose piece from falling. Awkwardly, I slid it aside and rested it on the roof. I put my head in first to try to determine the best way to enter. One of the pillars made from gods stood directly in front of me and I looked into the petrified eyes of a beautiful, silver-skinned nymph. "Sorry," I said as I hurled the spear at her. It sank home with a soft clunk, and I put my hand out and pulled myself inside.

## CHAPTER THIRTY-FOUR

I clung onto the side of the pillar with my spear in hand and ignored the fact that I was about two inches from what might be construed as a make-out session with a dead god. Because it was comprised entirely of corpses, the pillar provided many uneven surfaces for me to use as handholds. Once I'd stowed my spear on my back, I started to clamber down. I could have been more careful about it, but most of my brain and common sense had been swamped by my need to reach Deacon. It was hard not to picture the way his face looked in the mirror—so full of pain and suffering.

In my heart, I had known immediately that he was dying but I refused to accept it. I was determined that his death would not become a reality. He was the one person I absolutely could not lose.

I maintained a half-wary lookout for guards during my hurried descent and landed to push myself immediately into a run. No footsteps charged after me, so I didn't bother to look back. As I darted out of the central hall, I yanked the mirror shard from my coat pocket and looked at it. Deacon was there but only for a split second. He vanished in an instant.

"Come on, come on," I muttered under my breath. "Show me where they are." The image lurched to reveal a glimpse of a doorway recessed into one of the walls. The frame had a distinct pattern that set it apart from the surrounding wall. I glanced up in the exact instant in which I raced past it.

*There!*

My boots actually squealed to a stop. I flung myself at it and shoved against the door itself with all my might. It had no visible handle and it didn't budge at all. "Fucking move!" I demanded. My face flushed with exertion and frustration and all my power channeled into the barrier. The blood raged through my veins.

At last, it creaked open—not very much, but it was sufficient. I squeezed through that gap so fast, I almost tumbled down the steps directly behind it. These descended into a weird, rounded dungeon room. Blood-stains pooled and manacles littered the floor and walls. Otherwise, the chamber stood empty.

I froze for a moment and strained to hear over my own heart pounding and heavy breathing. No sound rewarded my attempt. Scraps of material were scattered on the floor around my feet, and I bent to pick one up. My fingers brushed a swatch of red leather and I cursed.

*What did you find?*

"This is part of Jules's jacket," I said. "She's had it since college. I'd know it if I was fucking blindfolded."

The rage swelled within me once more. I spun and

moved back the way I had come, taking the curving staircase two steps at a time. Every passing minute challenged my ability to remain stealthy more and more. It would undeniably help me to remain undetected, but I also welcomed the idea of a fight.

The center hall was still empty when I came back in. I was at the back now, and to my right was the door from which Delano had emerged before. It was ornately carved with portraits of eyes, snakes, bats, and twisted trees that bore dark and ominous fruit. I grabbed the heavy brass handle and pulled, even though I expected it to be locked.

It wasn't. The door swung back to reveal a study that oozed luxury. The back wall housed a gigantic window that provided a view of only barren cornfields. The space in front of it was dominated by a sleek black desk, its surface spotlessly clean. The chair was missing, but a tall, humanoid figure dressed in black lingered on the opposite side, silhouetted by the light that streamed in through the glass.

I drew my spear and shifted it in my hands. The moment of truth was upon me. I walked forward and opened my mouth to issue a challenge.

The man turned, and the words stuck in my throat. He wasn't Delano at all.

"Deacon?" My hands began to tremble. "What…what the hell happened to you?" His face was unmistakable, but the rest of him screamed an obvious contradiction. Heavy dark wings sprouted from his broad shoulders and horns curled from the sides of his forehead. He stared at me through eyes as black as night, like Brax's. All the warmth they had always held was gone.

"You know what happened," he said. I winced. He still had his own voice, but each word rode an edge of ice. "Say it. I want to hear you tell me what I am."

My insides swam in a cold, churning soup. I didn't want to capitulate to his demands, but more than that, I didn't want to fight him. I licked my lips. The words moved like molasses on my tongue. "He made you an Apprenti," was what I finally stammered into the unbearable stillness between us. "Deacon—"

"What did you expect?" He strode forward and slammed his hand down on the desk. "You abandoned us, Vic. I jumped in front of that blade to save you—to buy you time—and you repaid me with cowardice. I forced him to spare your life, only for you to run away. You left us to die." The force of his anger glowed from the depths of his demon eyes with an unearthly light. He had never been angry at me. Not like this.

"I'm sorry," I said. "We stood no chance."

He glowered but his ire seemed to die down. I watched him straighten the lapels on his suit the same way he had so many other times. "No," he said. "You're right. We didn't. We were pathetic little sacks of meat and bones who played at games far too large for us to comprehend. But Delano took pity on me. He showed me the truth, Vic."

"Oh, no." A searing knot formed in the back of my throat. "Deacon, no."

He continued as if I hadn't spoken at all. "Power is the true path," he declared. A slow smile bloomed across his features and the effect was uncanny. He looked like a mocking caricature of himself. "It's the only way. If we stay as we are and continue to foolishly pursue our small-minded human goals, we will be doomed to repeat the same cycles forever—or until we are exterminated. Whichever happens first." He moved around the desk toward me. "But Delano is proof that we don't need to be tethered to a miserable existence. He was human too."

"I know." I spoke softly. To even look at Deacon was horribly painful, and yet I couldn't tear my gaze away. How could this have happened?

He spread his arms wide. "And look at him now. All of this for a man who was once a simple Apprenti, like me."

"You're not a fucking Apprenti, you asshole!" I burst out. Tears welled in my eyes but I held them back. "You had a choice."

Deacon advanced on me, his clawed hands balled into fists. "You left me none," he said.

*Victoria.* Marcus's voice was low and somber in my head. I knew what he would say before he said it. *Although it is difficult, you must kill him. The Deacon you know is gone, replaced by a fiend who cannot—and must not—be trusted.*

The tears escaped and slid down my cheeks. "I can't," I said. "I can't."

Deacon leapt for my throat. I dodged to the side and he managed only to knock my arm. The spear burned fiercely in my grip and washed his face in fiery light. His eyes reflected nothing. They remained empty and hard, trained on me as he swung at my head.

"Deacon!" I parried his strike with the spear. Part of his jacket sleeve burned away and exposed grey-tinted skin. He hissed. "Stop, I don't want to do this."

He smirked. "It's too late, sweetheart. You should've thought about that while you ran away with your tail between your legs." His tone made the phrase sound vulgar. "All that's left to do is reap what you sowed. Let's get this over with, shall we?"

His massive wings beat to create a wall of wind that slammed me back toward the study door. I drove the point of the spear into the floor. The good old golden shield sprang up around me, and the wind sheared away as Deacon lunged.

Inside the protective dome, I waited with my hand on the spear and tracked the arc of his jump. At its zenith, I yanked the spear from its anchoring point. The shield exploded up and out and he was caught in its concussive shockwave, his momentum redirected toward the wall. I thought it would knock him out. I was wrong.

The bastard impacted with the marble and still landed on his feet. He brushed dust from his suit as he straightened. In a flash, he was on me again. The wings made it feel like he towered over my head until he picked me up by the neck. "Better than I thought," he admitted. "But not good enough."

I kicked fiercely at him and clawed at his face with one hand. The other tried in vain to loosen his grip. Deacon had been strong in his normal form but with the addition of Apprenti powers, he might as well have held me up with an iron vice. The edges of my vision greyed out. I felt my eyes bulge from the pressure.

"How does it feel?" he sneered and drew me in closer. "I guess I should really thank you for helping me to understand why Delano loves to watch the life drain from people's eyes. I have to admit, it's enthralling."

I responded by kicking him in the balls as hard as I

possibly could. He dropped me and doubled over.

"Yeah," I said and coughed around a ragged breath. "Delano didn't think of that shit, did he? Fucker." I still loved Deacon deeply, but I had no issues with a few choice curses after he'd made a frighteningly powerful attempt to choke the shit out of me. He rolled onto his side, protecting his groin. It was my turn to walk up on him.

"You deserved that," I told him. "Quit being a dick."

He groaned and grabbed at me. I dipped nimbly to the side and knocked him away with the spear. Another portion of his sleeve vaporized. He surged upward to pull me off balance, but I was ready. Half a second later, I had him pinned and he grunted as he attempted to thrash himself free.

"Damn dirty fighter," he growled.

I smiled sweetly. "You used to love that about me." It hurt my heart to banter this way with Deacon like he was merely another disposable vamp. But if I stopped to think too hard about where I was and what I was doing, I knew I'd freeze. He had made it abundantly clear that I shouldn't trust him to be merciful.

*Now, Victoria,* Marcus insisted. *Do it. Be strong.*

I clutched the spear and held it above his heart. Deacon smiled up at me. "You look exactly like him," he said.

I scowled. "Fuck you." Stupidly, unable to resist a sudden compulsion that swept over me, I dropped the spear and kissed him. His whole body went rigid. The claws on his hands tore at my coat. It was, I thought with some vague logic, much like kissing a charged wire.

Until he kissed me back.

The change that spread through him was ethereal and

strange. Something unspeakable fled from him and seemed to dissipate into the chamber. We lay together on the study floor for what seemed like a lifetime of forevers, our lips locked firmly together. When I made myself pull back for air, his eyes opened.

They were brown.

"There you are," I said fondly.

He said. "I'm sorry, Vic. Shit, I'm so sorry." Deacon sat up and wrapped his arms around me. "It was me talking, but it wasn't me. That sick son of a bitch had me trapped in my own head."

I nuzzled his neck. "Don't worry about it. I'm simply glad to have you back."

"I'm glad to be back." He ran his fingers gingerly through my hair. "Real glad."

Marcus cleared his throat. *In this case, I am more than happy to have judged in error. But I hope you have not forgotten the deranged god who is no doubt still searching for you.*

"Ugh," I said. "*That* guy." I climbed off Deacon and stood. "Stay here. I'm gonna go take care of our big problem in little Indiana."

"No way." He pushed to his feet. "Last time I left your side, I ended up looking like Dracula's understudy. We'll do this one together."

I smiled at him. "I always hoped you'd be open-minded enough to say that."

On the other side of the study door, which had closed in the struggle, a booming voice echoed across the central hall. It was so loud, I barely understood what he had said, but we both knew exactly who had spoken.

I wondered if the whole damn world could hear him.

## CHAPTER THIRTY-FIVE

"Be careful," Deacon cautioned. We stepped into the hall and kept our heads low. Delano's voice permeated the whole chamber. He was talking about a grand vision and rebuilding the world from its fetid ashes, or some shit like that. I found it difficult to be too upset about anything now that I had Deacon's hand safely back in mine. Suddenly, I was positive we could take on two Delanos and beat both to a pulp.

We would have to be creative, though. The only exit I knew of lay directly ahead and I no longer needed to act recklessly and out of my mind. I tugged on Deacon's arm and made an upward motion. "Let's check the roof out."

He raised an eyebrow. "The roof?"

"Yeah. You know. We can look at the stars. And the cornfields. And the dozens of gods who want us dead."

He laughed. "Well, shit. I didn't realize you were such a romantic."

I led him up the pillars and once again ignored the bodies I scrambled over.

*Victoria, I have a question,* Marcus said. *Forgive me if it is too personal. You are not required to answer.*

"Shoot," I said. "If it's about Deacon, he can't hear you anyway, so you're fine."

*I only wish to know how you deduced that kissing him would return his mind.*

"Oh." I shrugged while I continued to climb. "That's easy. I didn't. It was a total shot in the dark." A loose strand of hair fell into my face and I brushed it away. "But I remembered learning that Delano had cut his heart out when he became Lorcan's Apprenti, and I knew Deacon could never do anything like that. All I did was remind him that he still had it and that I was still there."

*I see. I...believe that makes sense.*

"Humans are emotional beings at our cores, Marcus. You know that. Our identities lie in the ways we feel. I made him experience what he really felt for me, and what do you know? He came back."

*Perhaps a useful trick to remember for the future,* Marcus said.

"Ha ha." I rolled my eyes. "You think you're so funny because you live in a necklace and I can't hit you. Wait until the next time we're in Carcerum, buddy."

At the top of the pillar, we pulled ourselves over the lip of the hole I'd cut in the skylight.

Deacon looked down through the glass. "I can't wait until Delano eats it."

"You and me both," I agreed. On my stomach, I crawled across the roof to the highest point. The scene that unfolded took my breath away in the worst way possible. Hundreds upon thousands of captive humans and

Forgotten had been crammed into the holding pen, shoulder to shoulder. There wasn't enough room to turn around, let alone struggle or rebel. The guards that had circled when I broke out had been posted every few feet along the bars. They never shifted their gazes off the restless horde.

I, on the other hand, couldn't direct my eyes anywhere other than Delano. He'd moved and now sat at the bottom of the temple steps as he addressed his literally captive audience. Once I had my first good look at him, I saw that it wasn't only Deacon who had changed.

Delano had evolved into a repulsive creature. All sense of form had evaporated and birthed a hideous mountain of flesh. A ponderous belly protruded over thighs studded by strange, knobby appendages. Several arms bristled from his back and their attached hands grasped constantly at nothing. The face that was cold and beautiful a week earlier bore no resemblance to itself anymore. He turned toward us and displayed a mess of eyes, mouths, teeth. Threads of saliva spilled from his lips.

"Talk about a downgrade," Deacon muttered. "Looking nasty there, friend." He paused. "I guess we are all pretty nasty, huh. Sorry."

I leaned over and kissed him. "I think I'm already used to it."

He cocked his head to the side, puzzled. "I think that makes me feel better," he responded after a moment's thought.

Down below, Delano held the *Gladius Solis* in a hand with ten fingers on it. The blade swirled with darkness. His whole body rippled, and Delano thrust the weapon into the air. One by one, the gods bowed and the humans and Forgotten in the holding pen followed suit as best they could in the cramped space. I sensed no inkling of protest among those assembled. They all thought it was far too late, that Delano's plan had run its course without a hitch.

He laughed loudly and gloated over his subjects. "Good!" he roared. "Submit to me, my wretched servants. I dare you to defy my divine authority."

"Okay." I stood and shouted so he could hear me over the sound of his own voice. "I defy you, Delano."

I paused and allowed him time to parse the situation. His countless eyes probed in all directions. When they finally found me, I waved at him and smiled. His expression morphed from smug satisfaction into a whole range of feelings. Rage. Amusement. A touch of apprehension.

He recovered smoothly and amusement took over. "I hoped you might show your face around here again, deserter. In fact, you could say I had counted on it. Now the people you have forsaken will have the pleasure of watching me strip the flesh from your feeble skeleton. I will wear your living bones as a crown."

I raised my eyebrows. "Why make a crown when I'll take your head off anyway?"

Delano wasn't fazed in the least until I revealed the spear.

That made him falter visibly. Again, he recovered fast. "I have nothing to fear from you," he sneered. "A single human, alone in the face of the god to end all gods? I think not." His smug smile returned in full force. "Even a Solis weapon won't be enough to defeat an entire army of gods!"

"That much is true," I conceded and nodded. "Which is

why I've brought in an army of my own." Rather than give him time to react, I aimed the tip of the spear and threw it with all my strength. Delano heaved his grotesque shape out of its path but his evasion was irrelevant. I hadn't tried to hit him. The spear glided unimpeded to its real target—the center of the gate on the holding pen. Its lock shattered on impact and the gate blew open and thrust the guard detail aside.

Dead silence reigned. The humans and Forgotten, newly freed, exchanged glances of confusion. They still didn't dare to speak, so I did it for them.

"The gods have pitted us against each other for far too long," I began. Delano hunched, motionless and apparently stunned. "They wanted us to be as a house divided, unable to stand together and so unable to rise up in rebellion. But the days of dividing and conquering end right here, right now. Each one of you before me—be you human, vampire, Were, satyr, or centaur—has a choice to make. You can continue to live the way you are, cowed in fear and solitude by some bullshit, fucked-up god-monster. Or you can join me in the fight right now. We can be rid of assholes like him once and for all." I gazed out over the multitudes. "To me, the choice is as clear as day but I leave it up to you. Return to the Forgotten or step alongside me and reclaim your freedom. Reclaim your dignity and nobility."

They stared at me for a long while, then stared at each other. Finally, they turned as one to stare at the gods. Vengeful hunger blazed in the mob's collective eyes. And for perhaps the first time in their lives, the gods were undeniably afraid.

"Throw off the chains the gods have placed upon you!" I

shouted. "Let's show these fuckers the mighty wrath of Earth."

The last word echoed into a void. No one moved on either side. The long silence stretched painfully before someone in the front of the holding pen grabbed a rock and flung it at the gods. It was followed by another, and another, and another. A shout rang out—a lone voice cursing the gods. Soon, it was bolstered by countless others. The human-Forgotten front began to shift and hundreds of thousands poured onto the plateau.

"Kill them, you fools!" Delano screamed. His whole malformed body quivered. "Kill them! Kill them all!"

The other gods, half-galvanized by his frenzy, stumbled uncertainly to meet their foes, and all hell officially broke loose. I dropped over the edge of the roof and landed neatly fifteen feet from the monstrosity that had swallowed Delano. He turned his pulsing eyes to me. The sword raised up above his head, and his many legs readied themselves up for the charge.

He had been intimidating in his previous form, but now, he was mostly plain gross. It was the *Gladius Solis* I worried about. The first wound I'd received from that thing had yet to heal completely and I did not want to sustain another.

I craned my head back as Delano bore down on my position. The black sword sliced downward as anticipated. I put my hand out, summoned the spear, and caught the edge of the sword's blade across the shaft. It wasn't hot anymore but neither was it cold.

The sword simply reeked of evil.

# CHAPTER THIRTY-SIX

Delano bared his crooked fangs scant inches above my face. His mouth filled with rows and rows of teeth jammed in there in such numbers that they seemed to burst outward when he dropped his jaw. I gathered my strength behind the spear and shoved him backward. His extra arms pinwheeled to try to maintain his balance. "This is a fucking joke," I said to him and stepped forward as he staggered back. "Have you seen yourself? You don't look like the sum of all gods, Delano. You look like Frankenstein's experiment gone off the rails."

He shifted his ponderous girth and backed hastily around the temple wall. The *Gladius Solis* slashed haphazardly through the air and left a black, noxious trail wholly unlike the arcs of fire I was accustomed to seeing. Where the blade scraped along the earth, its black aura lingered. "Give it up, Delano," I called and followed relentlessly. "You're making Kronin's sword look bad."

"Kronin?" Delano roared with laughter. "Don't make me laugh, girl. Kronin knew nothing of glory." He paused to taunt me. The whole building quaked as one of my giant buddies slammed a god with an armored shell into the side. The carapace and the stone both cracked and dust shook loose from the eaves of the roof. Delano cast a worried glance into the shadows and turned to face me. He charged with the *Gladius Solis* poised to carve out my heart.

The tip of the sword drew sparks when it collided with my spear. Delano roared and struck repeatedly. He tossed the sword from arm to arm in an effort to catch me off guard but I danced around him, traveled with it, and dueled each arm in turn. They were as strong as they were creepy, and I only managed to slice one off at the wrist. It fell with its fingers curled in like a dead spider.

Delano hissed. Blood poured down the backs of his legs from the brand-new stump. Annoyed by the sensation of a dead limb, he calmly pulled the whole arm off and whipped it at me. I sliced it at the elbow joint in midair. "Come on," I said. "You can do better than that."

He glanced around and a sick little smile slid across his features. His skin had assumed a greasy yellowish sheen. "I won't have to," he said. The smile evolved into a giggle and from there into full-on maniacal laughter. It was at this point that I noticed that the other fight between humans and the Forgotten and the gods had closed in around us. In a matter of minutes, the swarm of chaos would overtake me and I'd risk losing him in the melee.

"Fine." I threw myself into a vengeful sprint. My trajectory aimed the point of the spear into the center of his distended abdomen. The spearhead became a white-hot streaking comet as I increased speed. "Have it your way, shit-face. I'll bring the party to you."

He evidently hadn't considered the effect that his monstrous proportions might have on his speed, which was shamefully slow. Still, I was about to learn that the mutant god was more in tune with his horrible vessel than I expected. At the last minute, much like a car that took a turn way too fast, he careened onto one foot and teetered precariously, threatening to topple the other way. His laughter still rang in my ears, but I was the one who emerged with a grin because he wasn't quite fast enough.

The spear met almost no resistance on its way into his stretched, overstuffed side. Delano shrieked. A plume of murky blood spurted from the wound and his extra limbs went crazy. I leapt back to avoid the worst of their frenzied defense and yanked the spear out as I moved. The blood pumped harder to coat the ground in pools of deep-red, viscous liquid. One of the gods slipped in it. He was immediately pounced on by an angry Were and had his throat torn open.

Delano glanced at me. His misshapen face was sallow now as the blood seeped from the maltreated vessel he had created from his body. "It was a mistake," he rasped, "for you to return." He coiled, pulled all his energy into his legs, and spun away, trailing a kite of blood. His grotesque shadow sailed up and over the lip of the roof. I pulled my throwing arm back and prepared to release the spear. He was in for a big surprise if he thought he would get off that easily.

The ground beneath me shifted and threw my balance off. I stumbled but regained my feet, intent on my pursuit of Delano's ugly ass until a wave of people and Forgotten crashed in around me and blocked the way.

"Fuck!" I yelled and fought furiously against the tide, but it was too strong. The former caravan was a body in motion; its inertia could not be stopped.

I turned in search of another way and felt much like I was in a human washing machine. The fight raged on every side, and as I pushed my way in the general direction of the temple, I caught glimpses of my badass friends as they faced the chaos head-on. Brax's hammer was missing, but he had somehow gathered a whole militia behind him who hung on his every command. They swarmed an earth god the size of an elephant and worked together to bring it to the ground with a stupendous crash. As I turned away, Brax called to Smitty, and a squadron of west coast Weres flooded in to protect Brax's team. The blacksmith and the demon nodded stoically to one another.

An enraged howl shredded the air. It emanated from a smallish, red-tinted Were whom I could have recognized in my sleep. As always, Hurricane Maya left a wake of utter destruction. She had, I noticed, learned to differentiate between allies and enemies without losing her trademark strategy of simply throwing her adversaries at one another. Gods sprawled around her like discarded old boxes. I couldn't tell if they were dead, unconscious, or merely dazed.

*Knowing Maya, I would bet that they won't get up anytime soon,* Marcus said.

"Good," I answered, spitefully. "Fuck 'em."

*Indeed,* he agreed. *Delano, however, remains at large.*

"Yeah, where the fuck did he go?" I raised my gaze to scan the roof but Delano was nowhere in sight. "Maybe he fell through," I said, half laughing. "We did put that hole in the skylight."

*He has probably returned to his quarters,* said Marcus. *I would not be surprised to know he has some tricks left.*

"Dammit." I stood still for a second too long, momentarily paralyzed by a bout of indecision. It felt wrong to leave the center of the fight behind like a general abandoning her troops. But I also knew without a doubt that since I was the one who had forged the spear in Carcerum, I needed to wield it. Anyone else would be crushed by Delano's might.

I stepped forward to resume my journey to the temple, only to be stopped by a rising wall of screams. The combatants behind me either scrambled or were tossed aside to make room for the massive beast who hit me in the back like a semi-truck. I pitched forward and barely managed to break my fall. A lumbering, rank shadow fell over me.

"Hello, you little witch," jeered the ogre and his nose wrinkled in disdain. "Surely you must remember me." He notched his knuckles under my chin. The skin stretched taut on my neck as he forced my head up. With his fist holding my jaw closed, the only reply I could muster was a decisive middle finger. He growled and increased the pressure. My jaw and the vertebrae at the back of my neck creaked audibly.

At that moment, a furry hand clamped down on the ogre's greasy, bald skull. The razor-sharp claws raked over his skin and released a trail of foul blood to the air. He only had a moment of fleeting horror as the first hand's mate latched onto the other side of his head and the two tore him in half from head to toe. Ogre blood sprayed across me in a fine mist. I closed my mouth and eyes tightly.

"What are you doing?" Maya roared. Her arms were bloody up to the shoulders with fur caked into it. "If I can remember my humanity on a daily basis, you can damn well save it." She pushed me toward the temple. "Go, go, go! We can handle things on our own." I picked myself up with a smile. She was very serious.

The sharp reports of a gun cut through the din. Steph and Frank broke through the ranks and dodged around a falling god. She grinned at me as she took pot shots without looking. "Vic!" she shouted. "Go after that living ball-sack. We have it covered here."

"Tell him Frank says hello!" the vampire added.

Steph flashed him a warning look. "Don't tell him that."

More gunshots snapped through the air. Another god fell dead where it stood, killed by an unseen assassin. If I squinted hard at the temple door, I thought there might be a glimpse of Amber, holed up in her makeshift nest with a huge grin on her face.

"Don't just stand there, Vic!" The newest voice made me whirl around. Jules leapt across the carnage and swung Brax's hammer as if it rained money instead of fire. She had a look on her face that I'd only seen in the courtroom before—raw, intense conviction. Clearly, those two had enjoyed a few discussions about the philosophy of violence, and so far, it looked like Brax had won. "You heard Steph," Jules shouted again. She made another mighty swing and a smallish woodland god, all leaves and delicate branches, catapulted out of her path. "Don't let him get away."

*It seems as though your friends know best, after all,* Marcus said.

"Okay, okay!" I gave the battlefield one last glance. My crew would hold it the hell down. Righty and Lefty, the two giants, hung on the outskirts and picked up any stragglers dumb enough to try to leave. "I get it," I said with a grin. "They don't need me." Pride swelled in my chest. I was still smiling as I turned toward the temple and broke into a run.

## CHAPTER THIRTY-SEVEN

This time, instead of sneaking around like a hunted animal, I brought the tide of hell into Delano's temple. No sooner had I taken the first two steps down the wide aisle of the center hall than the pillars on both the left and the right came to life. They spilled out of their uncomfortable, tightly bound formations and shambled toward me with obvious intent to fight. Fortunately, all that time in suspension had weakened them severely while I was at the top of my game.

The Solis spear blazed a vengeful trail and branded its permanent mark on every emaciated body. I kept a special eye out for the silver nymph with the hole in her face, whose terrified eyes I had gazed into not so long ago. The spear's intrusion had half blinded her and she attacked with a scream of rage, one eye uselessly opaque.

I plucked her out of the air like a fly on the tine of a fork. Her body dropped to rest with the others, completely free at last of Delano's control. I hardly considered myself a saint for dispatching so many of Delano's thralls, but I wouldn't lose sleep over it either. They had made their ultimate goals clear in no uncertain terms and it was my job to make sure those goals never reached fruition.

Still, there were a lot of those frail, desperate entities that scrambled madly for their second chance. A grotesquely beautiful arachnid goddess somehow managed to slip behind me and lunge at my back with her sharp, barbed front legs. The first sting burned on my neck but I was momentarily deafened by an inhuman death screech in my ear. As I turned and cringed away from the terrible shriek, Deacon pulled his claws from the thorax of the huge black spider.

He grinned at me and shook slime from his hands. "And that," he said, "is why you keep me around."

"I can think of a few other reasons," I answered.

There was nothing left of the pillars now. The temple floor was strewn with bodies and slick with innumerable shades of blood. The last surviving holdout, an archaic, uncanny, almost-human creature, fled halfway down the hall before the door at the back banged open and Delano swooped out.

He snatched the god in his flabby clutches, seized it with his innumerable pairs of hands, and sucked its life force dry. Like so many others, the remaining husk was tossed aside. A moment later, each crooked, jutted limb began to elongate and elevate his disturbing corpulence too high in the air. The limbs were imbalanced in strength and perhaps too weak to support his bulk. He swayed dangerously atop his new supports and maneuvered to face us. Deacon and I gaped at him, a reaction he mistook for shock and awe.

"Power," he said. His voice was uneven and warbled a little, bordering on incomprehensible. Whenever he spoke, a chaotic mix of teeth flashed in his mouth. "Strength." He raised his arms like bristles across his body. "I can feel it. I can taste it. So close. So sweet."

"So fucked," I said. "You know as well as I do that it's time to end this madness. And I'm right here, right now."

The god's many eyes narrowed into glittering slivers. His face had lost all sense of structure. It was now merely a mess of features squashed together in a way that would have been extremely unsettling if I hadn't been so determined to kill him from the get-go.

"Very well," he declared at long last. "As you wish. Let us settle this petty, meaningless score."

The whole time, he'd gradually inched forward and now lashed out with one of his huge new legs. I dodged its cruel sweep only to have to leap aside again as it impacted the wall. The impression it left in the stone was deep and wide. He was terrifyingly fast now, as well as terrifying in general. I honestly didn't want to go near him, but I knew I had to. The tip of my spear needed to bury itself all the way down into that black heart.

After a few minutes during which we danced around one another, Delano finally seized an opportunity to attack and the impetus forced the air violently from my lungs. I severed a few of his legs as he charged, and the uneven distribution of weight finally began to hinder him. He now walked with a crooked gait and jerked around like a broken marionette.

Before I could anticipate his next move, he reared back and flames brimmed at the corners of his mouth. He spat them directly at Deacon and me. I threw myself out of the way, not at all fazed that I landed prone on the floor of the temple. I expected one of those snaky limbs to wrap around me at any moment and braced myself to slice straight through the flesh. But Delano had chosen to take Deacon out of the game and he did so with one swift blow.

"Deacon!" I couldn't keep myself from calling to him as he slumped onto the cold floor. Delano pushed his former Apprenti away like a pile of trash. "Fuck you! I'll make you answer for what you did to him."

"What I did to him?" The monster made the closest approximation to a smile that he could. "Darling, I improved him. You should thank me for that skin, those horns, and his increased longevity. All he had to do was admit that I've been right all along." He tucked his head into his tank-like body and launched himself toward me like an artillery shell. I scored his flesh as he passed.

"You made him an Apprenti!" I yelled. "You took everything from him and made him empty promises." I charged at the god's grotesque form and hurled the spear from a distance. It stuck hard in a flesh crease on his side and more grape-hued blood trickled from the wound. The spear disengaged at my silent call and returned to my hand. "And for what, Delano? So he could defy you for real in the end anyway? Nice plan."

Delano frowned. "Humans are weak," he hissed contemptuously. "The earthworms of the universe. No magic, no strength, no speed. Nothing to set them apart from every other completely trivial race that's ever been created. I threw away the dreary chains of humanity so that I might have a chance to elevate myself and learn more about how to fix the regrettable circumstances of my birth. I yearned to be something greater."

I motioned to his whole face as I danced barely of his reach. "I'll be honest with you, man. This whole hybrid thing you have going on isn't actually greater. You went too far. You crossed like fifty lines. There's no way to get this back the way it was."

"Silence!" he bellowed. The array of hands snapped out again in an attempt to snatch me. "I wanted everything for Deacon. I would have treated him like my own, as Lorcan did for me. He had potential to learn the ways." He paused, then smiled. "That's not true. I wanted to hurt you as badly as possible. And I did, so it wasn't a total failure. That's my favorite thing about humans." He smirked. "They have so many soft spots."

"Shut up!" Even the mention of Deacon's ordeal still threw me into a rage. "What do you know about pain and weakness, you scumbag fucker? You were never fucking human. That's why you could give Lorcan your heart in the first place. Because you didn't need it. You were already empty."

If I had expected Delano to be offended or hurt, it was a naïve hope. He beamed with pride instead. "Perhaps that is true," he admitted. "And what a wonderful Apprenti I was. Lorcan couldn't have asked for better, really."

"That's funny," I said. "Because we both know what happened to him."

A spark of anger flashed in Delano's eyes. He ran at me on those creepy, multijointed legs and tried to sweep me forward into a hug of death. His teeth gnashed relentlessly like a portable meat grinder that simply waited to chew me up. I didn't doubt for a second that he'd swallow me whole if he caught me.

But he now had a hard time adjusting to his latest modifications. The legs he had taken from the last god in the pillars slowed him immensely. He relied on far-reaching, area-of-effect attacks to keep me at bay, but I darted in and out of his personal space more quickly than he could strike.

We pushed and shoved our way out onto the front terrace of the plateau again, where the war still burned hot. Delano had his back to the fierce clash. He seemed to lose energy and patience. His body required massive amounts of fuel to function, and he realized that he'd eaten every god already—or, at least, the ones he could catch. His power seemed to be a finite resource, like a bright but short-lived star. The look in his eyes gradually shifted from supreme arrogance to something closer to anxiety.

"You will lose!" he screamed at me. "Why do you even fight? Not even Kronin could defeat me now."

I stared at the abomination in front of me, my spear leveled at his head. "You're right," I said. "Kronin couldn't win. But he fought his war with only half an army."

Delano's face contorted. "What is the meaning of that?" he demanded.

I pointed over his shoulder and waited patiently while he heaved himself around. The legs made small snapping sounds as if they had begun to break beneath his weight. Delano stared in silence. In the short period we had been outside, the fighting had petered out to a small skirmish here or there. The gods he had recruited were dead, gone, or captured. Every other eye atop that mountain now focused on him.

My crew stood stone-faced in the front and glared at him.

"It means I have all of Earth on my side," I said.

"No!" Delano whirled and lashed out with the sword. I swung my spear at the exact moment. The *Gladius Solis* shattered in his hand, an ignominious end to a noble weapon that had brought me so far. Before the pieces struck the ground, I leveled the spear at his chest. It burned brilliantly with Solis energy that thrummed to be released. The blast struck Delano right over the place where his heart had once been.

As heavy as he had become, Delano remained no real match for a Solis weapon. I watched him catapult back and be subsumed by the horde as if in slow motion. The last glimpse I ever had of him was his horrible, monstrous face and his mouth twisted open in a scream.

## CHAPTER THIRTY-EIGHT

"It isn't like this the first time," I said and paused on the side of the mountain to admire the crystalline blue sky. "It figures that the weather would behave better for an actual demon, I guess."

Brax laughed. "My reputation precedes me," he replied. He wore no special equipment for the climb, only his clothes and boots—and, of course, his glasses—and carried his hammer on his back. On mine, I carried the Solis spear. On my belt were the broken pieces of the *Gladius Solis.* The two of us had embarked on a special mission at my request. Months after Delano's fall at the temple in Indiana, we now headed to Carcerum one last time.

I didn't expect that there would be much to see there. Most of the deities who came to Earth had been at the temple that day, and the vast majority had fallen in the fight. The handful of survivors had fled or surrendered, which meant that the great halls of Carcerum still stood empty in their grandeur. We had considered the possibility of returning the few gods who were left to the home where

Kronin kept them, but as acting head of the brand-new Human-Forgotten Alliance, Jules objected.

I remembered that day as though it had happened minutes before, so vivid was the arguing, the passion, and the bickering. The other members of the Alliance, better known as the rest of my crazy friends, couldn't agree on where to send the last living gods. Dan and Veronica thought that since Carcerum had been set aside for them, that was where they should return but under different supervision. Frank and Steph yelled at each other about whether or not gods deserved to be treated humanely. Luis sat back, shook his head, and grinned silently.

Jules and Maya, however, had a new solution.

"Let's send them to Asphodel," the Were had said. Faced with a host of puzzled stares, she elaborated. "Look, what they've done is completely reprehensible. No one can dispute that. But if we simply stick them back in their happy golden fantasyland where they have everything they could possibly want, they won't learn squat. And maybe they'll multiply somehow, and maybe in another few millennia, they'll be pissed about something and this will happen all over again." She paused to let her words sink in. "If we put them in Asphodel, they will suffer. It might teach them some empathy, and if they have empathy, they might not act like such crazy jerks all the time."

"I agree, I think," Jules chimed in after a moment's thought. "I mean, I believe they deserve death, but we as humans are capable of mercy. Asphodel will be a place of repentance for them." She glanced at Brax. "Would you be willing to keep an eye on them while they serve their sentences?" Each god faced several centuries of time for literal crimes against humanity.

The demon had looked at her for a minute, classically impassive, and finally dropped his shoulders and started to giggle. The sound made us all a little uncomfortable, and it continued for a long time. But when the fit finally abated, he had agreed to be the jailer of Asphodel. He had also agreed, with some reluctance, to allow Jules to visit him on the weekends. When he told her it was too dangerous, she'd simply smiled and said, "Even jailers need conjugal visits."

I had never seen the demon shut his mouth so fast.

After that last meeting, we all went our separate ways for a while. Frank and Steph embarked on the most tempestuous, dramatic relationship we'd ever seen. The last I heard from them, they were on breakup number eleven, Frank planned to start a numbers racket with a gang of satyrs he'd met in the temple dungeon, and Steph vowed to shut them down before they even started.

Deacon and I went on cleanup duty and rounded up the last of the gods from the far corners of the earth. We found out from Namiko and others that a good number of them hadn't shown up to the final conflict. These beings proved to be mostly resigned to the whole situation, so we were able to take our time and have a vacation while we worked. We never really had the chance to relax together before that trip—not fully, anyway. A significant amount of time was spent in hotel rooms and he may have been tied up once or twice—by request.

Maya, in stark contrast to our debauchery-filled working vacation, continued to act as our moral backbone and dedicated her time to working with the newly freed Forgotten. She spent hours and hours at therapy centers and reached out to all kinds, but especially Weres. These learned how to deal nonviolently with their powers, how to control them, and how to channel them in a positive way. She was freaking amazing at it, to no one's surprise, and was uniquely qualified for the position.

Smitty and Amber traveled back to the Pacific Northwest after things stabilized in Indiana. Their camp inside a church exploded into a thriving community. Amber sent me pictures of a city in the early stages, minus skyways and buildings above the clouds. She said it was weird and wonderful to watch the place they'd built in the wilderness take on a life of its own. She still kept in touch with Namiko, who now ran all over the place and compiled every scrap of god-related information she could find. "Those who forget history are doomed to repeat it," she said. "We'll never forget about this again."

*Victoria.*

"Huh?" I snapped out of reverie and back into the clear, cold, sunny day. We were close to the summit, now, and perhaps an hour out from the peak. "What's up, Marcus?"

*I still do not understand the reasoning behind this return to Carcerum. It is a relic of history now. It serves no practical purpose.*

"Don't worry about it," I said as I'd done since the idea for the trip came into being. "It's no big deal. There's merely something I have to make right."

I stood by the forge in Carcerum and stared at the surface of the smithy. The broken pieces of the *Gladius Solis* lay arranged in front of me. They no longer swirled with Delano's black energy. His death had caused that influence to ebb over time. The telltale veins of orange had begun to return to the surface of the stone. With some skill and a lot of patience, I was certain the sword could be good as new.

But I wasn't there to repair it. I gathered the pieces and gave them to Brax, who melted them down in the forge's furnace. He removed the molten stone and poured it into the mold I had found. The shape of it was strange, ethereal, and foreign. If it didn't work, I told myself, it didn't work.

I had a feeling it would, though.

While the metal cooled, I removed Marcus's medallion and set it in there. The Solis Stone coalesced over top of the medallion and consumed it entirely. I drew a deep breath and looked to my left.

Marcus stood beside me in the flesh. He looked around, flexed his fingers, and patted himself down. "You could have restored anyone," he said to me. "Anyone you wanted. Yet you chose me?"

I shrugged. "Don't get all touchy-feely about it, okay? It has nothing to do with me or you, or whether I think you're super cool. Carcerum needs someone to stand watch, even if no one is here." I reached over my shoulder for the spear and withdrew the shard of the mirror from my pocket. I handed both to the old centurion.

"I'm sorry it broke," I said. "I hope you can fix it. And that you'll keep an eye on Earth."

Marcus bowed his head. "It would be my honor, Victoria." He paused. "What will you do now?"

I took a deep breath and glanced at the demon. In true Brax fashion, he offered nothing more than an unhelpful shrug.

"I don't know," I admitted. "But I'm through being the captain of the ship. It's time for someone else to step up to the helm."

"That is fair," said Marcus. "You have done so very much for this world and its people."

"I have one last request," I told him. "And you can't laugh."

"I will not," he swore solemnly.

I smirked. "Could I get a lift back to Earth? The door in the palace is like, *so* far away."

The Roman smiled in response. "This is a trick you never did learn." He raised the spear and used its tip to cut a perfect shining circle in space and time. I reached out, grabbed his free hand, and squeezed it tight.

Then, Brax and I walked on through.

# EPILOGUE

E ven the air smelled differently on the way down the old familiar street in Brooklyn Heights. The route wasn't nearly as busy as it had been only a year or so ago before I knew the word "Forgotten" had another meaning. But the big empty spaces and the slowed pace weren't unique to my old neighborhood. The whole city was like that now as it struggled back onto its feet from one hell of a dirty fight. JFK was the only major international airport up and running again, and even then, only a restricted number of planes could be cleared for takeoff and landing. Real conversations in the streets were rare but grateful smiles were common.

As New Yorkers, we all took a little of the responsibility to nurture our beloved city back to health. She would never look the same again—that much was undeniable— but she could stand tall and be strong. Her pulse could once again beat through the veins of her streets.

I loved the walk around my old stomping grounds,

despite the rubble that edged the streets and the fine white dust left by buildings that had collapsed months before. Enormous sections of the city remained uninhabitable, and popup shelters had sprung up everywhere to accommodate those on the streets. It warmed the cockles of my heart to see New Yorkers step out to help their neighbors during a time when nobody had much of anything.

Lost in my thoughts, I turned from the main thoroughfare onto my street. Green buds had begun to explode on the trees that had managed to survive. Patches of vibrant blue sky showed through the wiry branches. The sun shone brightly although still without too much warmth. All in all, it was a nice day in New York again.

*Freaking finally.*

I approached Mac's newspaper stand and hoped against hope that the old guy would be there. He wasn't and the stack of gradually yellowing papers on his counter was months old, but I still took one off the top and fished a wrinkled dollar from my pocket to leave as compensation. Out of habit, I glanced up and down the street to see if I'd missed him chugging along on his way to open after a suspiciously long smoke break. Mac was nowhere to be found. I hoped he was okay.

The paper was tucked under my arm as I resumed my leisurely stroll toward the shitty apartment building I'd lived in for so long. No Sam lounged under his hat in front of the door, either. A bittersweet pang of nostalgia kicked me in the chest. I wanted to think that Sam and Mac might have moved on and found something else to do or somewhere else to be. I could imagine them trekking through the Forgotten-ravished landscapes I had seen, smiling and drinking in each other's serene guidance. It was a nice daydream, anyway, but there was no way to disguise the reality that things were tough and they would be for a long time. We were tougher, though. We humans would persevere because after all, some things never changed.

I stepped through the same front door with the rickety overhead light and checked the plastic dome for the same large moth that had laid dead in the bottom for centuries. It was there, and so were the rusty mailboxes that never locked, all predictably hanging wide open. I took the steps to my old apartment on the top floor, which was also unlocked.

It smelled musty and close in there. The first thing I did was go to the windows and yank them open. The place was an absolute wreck. Inches of dust blanketed items that had lain unattended for months. Pieces of my walls and broken furniture littered the floor—leftovers from any number of confrontations, I was sure. Clutter heaped high on the only table. The hot plate was in need of a good scrubbing. A weird smell wafted from the depths of the mini-fridge. The bathroom corner didn't even have a damn door.

Ignoring all that, I cleared the sofa off with a wide sweep of my arm, sat, and sighed as I collapsed into the cushion. It was like a welcome-home hug, and it felt amazing. Then something strange and furry touched my elbow, and I almost screamed bloody murder.

The cat poked her nose out from behind the couch and jumped up next to me. She was a little scrawny, but she seemed otherwise healthy.

"How'd you get back here?" I asked. I hadn't seen her since before we'd first arrived at Fort Victory. She meowed at me and purred like a motorcycle engine as she leaned into my hand for scratches and ear rubs. I let her tuck under my chin as I opened the paper. It was all as weird as hell and way too ordinary.

I kind of loved it—at least, for now.

The knob on the janky apartment door turned and Deacon stepped through. He was a vision in a suit, a look that was only enhanced by his other, more unique attributes, as far as I was concerned. After Delano had fallen, many of his more overt demonic features had faded somewhat. I had to say that decent clothes and regular showers really helped. It was hard to believe, but he looked much like he had when he was fully human. He'd reclaimed most of his sleek, sharp style. And of course, he was still the same Deacon I tried so hard not to fall for once upon a time.

"Hey, gorgeous." He sat himself down on the sofa beside me and worked his arm gently around my waist. I shifted my weight against his chest and settled into the warm contours of his body. "What are you reading?"

"The wanted ads from, like, six months ago," I said. "I figure it's about time I got a real job, you know? Maybe start thinking about building a real life."

Deacon laughed. "You have a funny sense of timing, sweetheart. Money doesn't seem all that important at the moment. Who knows when we'll have a working economy again?"

I flipped the page and snuggled deeper into his arms. "It's not really about the money. I want to set a good example."

He turned his head down to look at me, confused. I

took his hand, the skin still vaguely blue-gray toned and the talons on his fingers neatly trimmed, and I placed it over the middle of my stomach. There were no kicks to feel yet, but there would be soon enough.

I smiled at him. "For the next generation."

Dearest readers,

I've been putting off this set of author notes for a couple of days now. Not because I don't love our little chats, but because we've reached book eight.

Vic and friends have won the battle, and it seems that her crew is assembled to watch over a new *Pax Terra*—Peace on Earth.

Ending a series is tough for Lee and me. In fact, out of three full series we've written, this is the first one that we've decided needs to have a decisive close. Even as I write this, I keep wanting to hedge my bets, leave an open door for future books in the world of *Forgotten Gods*. But, lo and behold, I won't.

Am I going to promise that we will never, ever come back and write more stories about Vic, Deacon, Maya, and the rest of the crew? Hell no!

One never can tell where the winds will blow our creative juices, but let's all enjoy the victory, exhale, and continue on to the next series to fall in love with—and we have some for you!!

It's been a little over a year since Lee and I pitched the idea of the gods' return to Michael Anderle, and since then, we've become completely smitten with the characters, the world, and all that Forgotten Gods had to offer.

This has been a really fun run... but I want you to know, the most incredible part of the process is you!

There are authors out there that write their words for the love of the craft. I hear people say they could write their books for an audience of none. Do I get that? Um... sort of. But the truly fun part of it all, what really gets us grinding away through the midnight hours and during lunch breaks and while I wait for my kids at practice is YOU.

So, in this last note in this series, I want you to know that we are forever grateful. We love our readers—those we've heard from over the years, as well of the ones we'll never get a peep out of.

Finally, we started in the world of writing as what is known as "indie authors." Independent. Self-publishers. But there is nothing "independent" or "selfie" about being an author, whether you're in the traditional world or not. That's why we need to offer a big final thank you for the team that surrounds us as well. To the Just in Time reader team, editors, administrative staff, and our incredible cover designer (Hey, Heather!). It's always a team production, and there were many, many people doing the heavy lifting on this one.

Oh, there's one last person to thank: ST Branton.

All this time, ST has been tied up in Lee's basement,

wedged between the water heater and a pile of self-help books writing away. He's a heck of a guy. Almost never complains. A saint, really (get it?).

You might be wondering if we're letting ST out now. Not a chance! He's already writing outlines and beats for our next Urban Fantasy, and we are really, really excited about it.

We think you will be too! The working title is *The Heinous Crimes of Sarah Slick...* Here's the tagline: "She's the human that monsters fear at night." If all goes well, it will be out in the Spring of 2019. Keep your head up and eyes open!

Thanks again for taking the journey with us.

For Kronin,

Chris (and Lee)

PS: We have heaps and heaps of books for you to read and three projects currently nearing publication.

If you want to get updates in your mailbox, sign up here: https://www.subscribepage.com/chris_and_lee (you also get a fun, fast sci-fi thriller for free!).

PPS: If you've loved Vic and friends, we really think you'll fall fast for Hannah in our Rise of Magic series.

Grab the Box Set of the first four books for one low price (or free on Kindle Unlimited)

**Steel City Heroes Saga**

**The Catalyst**
Buy The Catalyst

**The Crucible**
Buy The Crucible

**The Casting**
Buy The Catalyst

**Jack Carson Stories**

**The Devil's Due**
Buy The Devil's Due

**The Devil's Wager**
Buy The Devil's Wager

**The Rise of Magic**
* With Michael Anderle *

**Restriction (01)**
**Reawakening (02)**
**Rebellion (03)**

# CONNECT WITH CM RAYMOND AND LE BARBANT

**Email List:**

www.subscribepage.com/smokeandsteelnews

**Facebook:**

Come hang out on the Forgotten Gods Facebook page:
www.facebook.com/ForgottenGodsSeries/

**Website:**

www.smokeandsteel.com